# Natural Reaction

## A MARY O'REILLY PARANORMAL MYSTERY

by

Terri Reid

## A note from the author:

Although this is a work of fiction, post-traumatic stress disorder (PTSD) is a real illness. You can get PTSD after living through or seeing a traumatic event, such as war, a hurricane, rape, physical abuse or even a bad accident. PTSD makes you feel stressed and afraid after the danger is over. It affects your life and the people around you. You are not crazy, you are not weak, and your mind is just reacting to the mental and emotional trauma, just as your body would react if the trauma had been physical. You wouldn't call yourself weak if you broke your arm and needed a cast, would you? Get help. Talk to someone. Don't let this event rule the rest of your life.

NATURAL REACTION – A MARY O'REILLY
PARANORMAL MYSTERY

by

Terri Reid

Copyright © 2011 by Terri Reid

The author would like to thank all those who have contributed to the creation of this book. The editors: Debbie Deutsch, Jan Hinds, Ruth Ann Mulnix and Tonja Rieke. The invaluable assistant: Sarah Reid. The proof-reader and husband: Richard Reid.

And especially to the wonderful readers who walk along with me through Mary and Bradley's adventures and encourage me along the way. Thank you all!

# Prologue

The bell pealed its final warning and two dozen high school students quickly rushed in from the grey locker-walled hallway into the chemistry lab. But even though they were in his classroom, Charlie Thorne, their teacher, knew they were more concerned about the upcoming Spring Fling than anything else. "Okay, ladies and gentlemen," he yelled over the clamor of voices. "I need you to quiet down and pay attention."

"But Mr. Thorne," bubbled Rosie Meriwether, the Homecoming Queen and a shoo-in for Prom Queen, "they just announced the band for the Spring Fling is going to be The Nomadds."

"And yet they still allowed classes to continue," he teased.

"Coach Thorne," Stevo Morris, the shortstop for the high school baseball team Charlie coached, said. "This is a really big deal. The Nomadds are cool."

"Thank you, Stevo," Charlie replied. "And as *cool* as they are, the only cool we are going to discuss today are endothermic reactions."

A low groan was emitted from the students and Charlie chuckled. "Cheer up," he said. "Today's experiments are fun and if you get them right, you

1

won't have to write the fifteen-page paper on displacements instead of going to the Spring Fling."

The class was immediately alert and quiet. "Yeah, I thought that would work," he laughed.

He moved to the front of his lab table and looked around the room. He was younger than most of the teachers in the school by at least ten years. Because of his good-natured personality, he was a favorite among the students. But he would be surprised to know that he was also considered the "dream man" for many of the high school coeds.

"Okay, Stevo, explain single displacement," he said.

Stevo grinned. "You mean the Raquel Welch Displacement Theory, sir?"

Charlie nodded. "Yes, that's the one."

"Okay, so I walk in the classroom with Raquel Welch on my arm," he explained. "And then we walk over and meet you, right? So, she sees you and ditches me for you, because you're a studlier element or a more active element."

Charlie nodded and chuckled. "Exactly, single displacement," he said. "She leaves Stevo for me because, well, she has good taste…"

The class laughed at his joke.

"And because I am a more active element than Stevo."

"Except in practice when we run laps, coach," Stevo added. "Then I'm more active."

Charlie nodded. "And that's why I'm the coach and you're the shortstop."

He walked over to the chalkboard and wrote:

$$NH_4OH + HNO_3 = NH_4NO_3 + H_2O$$

"This is an example of the Raquel Welch, Brigitte Bardot Double Displacement Theory," he explained. "It's the same premise, except instead of just one active element replacing a less active element, there are two separate changes going on here. In this case, I am the ammonium ion and I replace the positive hydrogen ion from the nitric acid, $HNO_3$ and bond it to me. The remaining Hydrogen ion is left with the OH and becomes $H_2O$ or…"

"Water," Rosie called out.

"Exactly. Water," Charlie replied. "So, applying that to our theory, Raquel and I are together in this classroom."

He circled the N. "Nitrogen."

Then he circled the H. "Hydrogen."

"Then Stevo walks in with Brigitte Bardot on his arm," he added, as he circled $NO_3$. "She takes one look at me and leaves Stevo and hooks up with me and Raquel. And Stevo is left with…"

"Water," the class replies.

Charlie laughed. "Exactly, Stevo is left with water."

He moved back to the front of the lab table. "Okay, first a big hand for Stevo for being a good sport."

The class broke into a round of applause and Stevo stood and bowed.

"Now, next we are going to have some fun with chemicals," he said. "The experiment I just showed you is how to make ammonium nitrate. Who knows what that's used for?"

Jonathon MacComber, one of the boys who lived out in the country, raised his hand.

"Yes, Jon."

"It's fertilizer," he said. "We use it all the time."

"Yes, you're right. Excellent," Charlie responded. "Because of the high concentration of nitrogen, farmers use it to increase plant growth. However, combining the ingredients to make ammonium nitrate can be a little tricky, so I'm going to demonstrate how to do it and then I'll let each of you use some ammonium nitrate to perform a cool experiment."

Charlie pulled a tray of sealed glass bottles and a couple of empty beakers to the middle of the table. "Okay, I want you to all put on your safety glasses because this stuff gets hot and can splatter."

He put a 550 mL beaker in the middle of the table and then opened one of the glass bottles. "First, I'll put 100 mL of water into the beaker. Stevo, you remember about the water, don't you?"

Stevo chuckled. "Sure do, Coach."

Charlie opened the next bottle. "This is nitric acid," he said. "You always want to add acid to water because if you do it the other way around, the acid will splash up when the water is added to it."

He reached over for a metal bowl that was filled with water and ice. "Okay, the next ingredient is ammonium hydroxide, but before we start adding it, we are going to place the beaker into a salt-ice bath because this stuff really heats up when it's mixed together."

Placing the beaker into the bowl, he opened the bottle of ammonium hydroxide and started to slowly add it to the mixture. "I'm using a piece of litmus paper to test when the ingredients become alkaline and I'm slowly adding the ammonium hydroxide so it doesn't come to a boil. Jon, come on up here and lightly touch the beaker."

Jon came up and placed his fingertips on the beaker. "Whoa, that stuff is hot, Mr. Thorne."

"Yes, the chemical reaction is causing the molecules to move quickly which is creating heat."

A few minutes later, Charlie moved the beaker out of the ice water and over to the Bunsen burner. "Okay, now that it's reached an alkaline level, I will boil off the rest of the water and only a crust of white will remain. That crust is ammonium nitrate. So Stevo is boiled away and I am left with Raquel and Brigitte."

He set the beaker to the side and lifted the safety glasses off his face. "Any questions?"

Stevo raised his hand. "So, which one are you taking to the Spring Fling and can I have the other one?"

The students laughed along with Charlie. "In your dreams, Stevo, in your dreams."

He moved the tray to the side and pulled out a stack of mimeographed paper. "Okay, here's your lab assignment. You are going to be mixing ammonium nitrate with water to create an endothermic reaction."

"So, that hot stuff is going to get cold when you mix it in water?" Jon asked.

Charlie grinned. "Well, that's for me to know and for you to find out. Go with your partners to your lab tables and remember to keep your safety glasses on. Even though this is a very safe experiment, we never want to take chances."

He walked around the room, handing out the instructions and making sure each student had their safety glasses and lab smocks on. "Okay," he said. "Take a spoonful of the ammonium nitrate and place it in the beaker. Now open the brown bottles of distilled water and slowly pour it onto the powder..."

"Wow! This really works," Jon said. "It's like freezing."

"Good job, Jon," Charlie said, applauding the student. "You have just created an endothermic reaction."

"Does that mean I get to take Raquel Welch to the Spring Fling?" he asked with a grin.

"Not in this lifetime," Charlie responded.

"Hey, Coach, something's wrong with my experiment," Stevo called. "It's like foaming up and getting hot."

Charlie quickly turned. "Stevo, step away..."

Before he could finish the sentence, the beaker had exploded and the lab table was on fire. "Everyone, out of the room," he yelled, running to the fire extinguisher.

He pulled it off the wall and ran to the table. Pressing the handle, he waited for the white foam to burst from the nozzle, but nothing happened.

"Coach, the door is locked," Stevo called, panic obvious in his voice. "I can't open it."

Charlie ran to the door and tried it. Stevo was right, it was locked. He tried throwing himself against it, but the solid wood door was not going to give. He glanced over his shoulder and saw the fire spreading to the next lab table. Another small explosion of glass and wood had the students screaming in fear.

"Okay, okay, calm down," he said. "Everyone over to the window."

"But Mr. Thorne, we're on the second floor," Rosie protested. "That's too far to jump."

"Don't worry, Rosie," he said. "We'll make it work."

He moved the students to the very front of the classroom. The fire was quickly spreading throughout the back and moving forward. He opened the window and looked down. The evergreens below the window would break most of the fall, but they would still need to be helped down.

"Stevo, you take the next window. Okay, I want you to hold our hands, we'll reach down as far as we can and then you can drop onto the bushes below. The first ones down, help the next ones. We have to work together and we have to move quickly."

Charlie picked two of the taller boys to go first, so they could help the others on the ground. He and Stevo held on to them until they had reached as far down as they could and then let them go. The boys dropped onto the bushes and rolled off. Charlie breathed a sigh of relief when both boys jumped up, unhurt.

Stevo turned to Charlie and smiled. "They made it, Coach, they made it."

"Yeah, they did. Now let's get the rest of the class out of here."

Although they moved quickly, the fire moved faster. The last few students climbed through windows that had black smoke also billowing out of them. Finally, Stevo and Charlie stood alone in the room. "Come here, Stevo," Charlie said. "I'll let you down first."

"But Coach, who's going to help you?"

"Hey, you're my best fielder, I expect to jump right into your arms," he said. "Just promise not to whip me over to Smith for a double play."

The young man, his face streaked with soot, grinned at his coach. "Yeah, Coach, I promise."

Charlie took the young man's hands in a tight grip and slowly lowered him out the window. When he had extended his reach as far as he could, he let him go.

Stevo fell into the evergreen boughs, the prickly needles scraped his arms, but the branches kept him from hitting the ground. He rolled off the bushes and jumped up as fast as he could. He turned his eager face up to the window. "Okay, Coach," he called.

The explosion violently blew the windows out of the building. Screaming students darted across the lawn, barely escaping the shards of glass raining down on them. All of the students except Stevo, who still stood below the gaping hole in the wall, oblivious to the blood running down his face and arms. "Coach, Coach," he screamed. "I'm here, Coach. Coach, I'm here."

## *Chapter One*

The hospital room was quiet, except for the sounds of the monitors recording Mary O'Reilly's vital signs. The air smelled of flowers from the dozens of bouquets distributed on every available space, with an underlying residue of lemon disinfectant.

Police Chief Bradley Alden paced back to the bed and gazed down at her. She still hadn't moved, hadn't shown any sign she was coming out of this unconscious state. *Could Sean be right? Could Mary be taken from me?*

His stomach clenched and a cold frisson of fear slipped down his spine. *How would I ever be able to survive without her?*

He sat on the edge of the bed, leaned forward and cradled her face in his hand, gently stroking her cheek with his thumb. "You are my heart, Mary O'Reilly," he said. "You can't leave me now. I love you."

He placed a soft kiss on her forehead and then brushed his lips across her cheek.

"Mary, will you marry me?" he whispered.

Tenderly placing his lips on hers, he kissed her with all the love he had in his heart, trying to force a response from her. Was it hopeless? Would he really have to live without her?

A single tear slipped from his cheek and landed softly on hers.

She suddenly took a deep shaky breath and her eyes opened slowly.

"Bradley," she whispered. "What did you say?"

Relief and elation surged through him; he wrapped his arms around her, pulled her close and was surprised when she stiffened and pushed against his chest.

"No, please, let me go," she cried, her voice panicked and halting.

He immediately stood up and moved slightly away from the bed. "Mary, it's me, Bradley," he said, trying to soothe her. "I'm not going to hurt you."

She scooted back in the bed, her back flush against the headboard, her eyes still wide in fear. "Bradley?" she asked, her gaze examining his face and then the room beyond him. "Where am I?"

"You're in the hospital, Mary," he said. "You're safe."

Her search became frantic. "My baby," she cried. "I heard my baby. What have you done with my baby?"

*What the hell?* he wondered. *What's going on?*

"Mary, you don't have a baby," he said, keeping his voice soft and low. "Jeannine had a baby."

"Jeannine?" she asked, recognition showing on her face. "Where's Jeannine?"

"She's moved on, Mary. You found the man who killed her. She's at peace now."

Wrapping her arms around her body, she began to tremble. "He kept me down there for so long," she sobbed. "He kept..." Her voice broke. "He kept touching me and no one came for me. No one saved me."

"Mary, I'm so sorry," he whispered, his heart filled with remorse.

He started to move forward, aching to hold her in his arms and protect her.

"No, no," she whispered, her head shaking back and forth. "Don't come closer, please don't come closer."

His heart sank and he took a deep breath. "I wasn't going to hurt you," he said. "I just wanted to comfort you."

Placing her hand over her mouth and with tears flowing down her cheeks, she shook her head. "I'm sorry, Bradley," she sobbed. "I just can't. I don't know what's happening, but I just can't."

The door opened and Bradley turned around quickly. No one was going to get close to Mary while she was so distressed.

"Ma," Mary called out, relief evident in her voice.

Maggie O'Reilly stood in the doorway for a moment to assess the situation. Bradley, who she knew adored her daughter, had several days' worth of stubble on his face and clothes so wrinkled she knew he'd slept in a hospital chair for more than a few nights. But it was the look on his face that had her curious. He looked both confused and hurt, as he stood next to Mary's bed like an avenging angel.

She turned to her daughter, huddled up at the top of her bed as if the big bad wolf was coming for her. She'd been crying, the tears still wet on her face. Something was certainly amiss.

She walked across the room, patted Bradley reassuringly on his shoulder and then moved past him to enfold Mary into her arms. "There now, little lamb," she crooned. "Your ma is here to take care of you."

"Oh, Ma," Mary sighed. "I'm so confused."

Maggie smiled up at Bradley. "Why don't you go get the doctor and give us a moment alone?" she suggested.

Bradley nodded slowly, his eyes still on Mary wrapped in her mother's arms. He hesitated.

"She'll be fine," Maggie assured him. "Now go get the doctor."

Once the door closed behind Bradley, Maggie stepped back and sat alongside Mary on the bed. "Now, why don't you tell me what's been going on?"

She pulled a tissue from the box on the table alongside the bed and handed it to Mary.

Shaking her head, Mary wiped her eyes and her nose, and took a deep wobbly breath. "I don't understand," she said. "I know Bradley would never do anything to hurt me. I know he's risked his life for me. But when I woke up and he was holding me, I

13

panicked. All I could think of was being down in that dark room and Gary touching me."

Her body trembled.

Maggie leaned forward and took Mary's hands in her own. "Now, you have to tell me," she said. "Did that man…?"

Mary shook her head. "No, Ma, he didn't rape me. But…it's hard to explain."

"I'm listening."

Mary nodded. "How much has Sean already told you?"

Maggie smiled. "Your brother told me about Bradley's wife and how you've been helping to solve her murder. He felt, perhaps, you put yourself more at risk than was wise."

"No, I only did what was necessary," Mary insisted.

"Spoken like a true O'Reilly," Maggie replied ironically. "Now, what is it that was necessary?"

"The only way we could help Jeannine remember what happened to her was to hypnotize her," Mary explained.

"I've never heard of a ghost being hypnotized before."

"That was the difficulty," Mary said. "She had to have a body in order to be hypnotized, so I let her use mine."

"You let a spirit into your body?" Maggie exclaimed. "Blessed Mother, do you know the risks of such behavior?"

She nodded. "I do," she said. "And we took precautions. But Ma, really, it was the only way."

Maggie closed her eyes for a moment and took a deep breath. "And then?" she asked, meeting Mary's eyes once again.

"And then Ian hypnotized us," she said, and then paused before adding. "And I lived through Jeannine's memories."

Maggie gasped softly. "So, that man did rape you."

Tears slid down Mary's cheeks again and she weakly shrugged her shoulders. "I don't know," she cried quietly. "He didn't touch me physically, but…"

"But you felt the emotions and…the pain?" she asked, her own eyes filling with tears.

Mary nodded. "Yes. Yes, I felt it."

Maggie leaned forward and held her daughter in her arms. "My darling little girl, I'm so sorry."

Inhaling deeply, Mary relaxed in her mother's arms. "I don't remember a lot of details. Jeannine was drugged for the most part. So my memory is foggy. But the fear and the feeling of complete helplessness are there, like something's waiting just around the corner."

"You need to talk to someone," Maggie said. "You need counseling."

Mary laughed humorlessly. "And just who could I talk to who wouldn't want to lock me up in an institution?" she asked.

"Mary, you have to get help," her mother insisted. "This is not something you can handle on your own."

Mary sat up, wiped away her tears with her sleeve and smiled bravely. "Ian said something about hypnotizing me and removing Jeannine's memories," Mary replied. "I'll try that first and then, if I can't do it myself, I'll get help."

Maggie frowned and shook her head. "Damn stubborn thick-headed O'Reilly," she muttered. "You'll help everyone but yourselves."

Mary smiled. "I love you, Ma."

Maggie pursed her lips. "And don't think you can use O'Reilly charm to get around me," she said. "Now, I've my things in the car and I'm planning on staying a while to make sure you get some help."

"I really appreciate the offer..."

"Are you throwing your own mother out into the cold streets?"

Mary chuckled. "No, I'm not. But I just can't let you do this," she explained. "I need to be strong. I need to rely on myself."

"Mary, since the time you could walk you relied on yourself. I'd never seen such a single-minded child. You had to be just as good as or better than your brothers," her mother said with a sigh. "This time it's okay to need someone else."

Mary took her mother's hands. "Ma, you've always let me be strong, let me be independent and I could because I always knew you were there, ready to pick me up if I fell down," she explained. "This time, it would be too easy to run to you and let you fight my battles for me. This time I really don't want to do it on my own. And that's the reason why I have to. I have to face this monster by myself. If I don't do it now, I think it could change me. I don't want to be afraid."

Maggie picked up one of her hands and pressed it against her lips for a moment. "You are a brave girl and you have more courage than should be allowed in a body your size. I understand what you're saying and I'll honor your wishes, under one condition."

Mary nodded.

"You call me, anytime, night or day, if you need your mother," she said firmly. "You promise."

"Yes, I promise," she agreed. "And just knowing you're there, just a phone call away, will be a comfort."

Maggie leaned forward and kissed Mary on her forehead. "There are others, even closer, who you can rely on too. Try to trust Bradley again. He's a good man and he loves you."

Mary kissed her mother's cheek. "Thank you, Ma."

The door opened behind them and Bradley entered. "Dr. Thorne is on rounds," he explained. "She'll be coming in as soon as she can."

Maggie gave Mary's hand a soft squeeze and then stood up. She walked over to Bradley and, tiptoeing, placed a kiss on his cheek. "You take care of my baby girl," she said.

"There's nothing else more important to me," he replied.

She looked up into his eyes and saw the truth in his words. "I know that," she said. "Help her to trust again."

Bradley nodded. "I will."

# Chapter Two

When the door closed behind Maggie, Bradley cautiously approached the bed. "I have to admit I'm a little unsure of things," he said. "I don't want to frighten you."

Mary nodded, took a deep breath and patted her bed. "Why don't we try having you sit down here next to me and then I'll try to explain things. But first, I have some questions."

Bradley sat tentatively on the bed, trying to give her all the space she needed. "Okay, what questions?"

"I remember the brunch; what happened next?"

"Gary drugged everyone and once they had all passed out, kidnapped you," he explained. "I was looking at the webcam and saw everyone passed out. I called the local police chief and had him check things out. When Jeannine realized that it was Gary and he had you, she immediately went to help."

Mary nodded slowly. "I remember Jeannine talking to me and I can remember glimpses of fighting Gary, but it wasn't me."

He shook his head. "No, you were drugged, but Jeannine was able to somehow enter your body and together you both kicked his ass."

She studied Bradley for a moment. "Okay, that's not exactly what happened, was it?" she asked. "What are the things you are leaving out?"

Sighing, he ran his hand through his hair. "When I found out Gary had you I immediately went to his home," he began reluctantly. "I searched the house and finally found a room in the basement."

"Was I in there?"

He shook his head. "No, there was a desk, a chair and an upright freezer, the room was pretty empty. I opened the freezer and found the remains of a woman wrapped in plastic."

Mary gasped, covering her mouth with her hands. "Who?"

"I thought it was Jeannine," Bradley said. "And then I found a box with the remains of an embryo."

Reaching out, she placed her hand on his arm. "You thought it was your daughter, didn't you?"

He nodded. "When I saw what he had done to Jeannine and my daughter, and then I realized he had you…"

Taking a deep breath, he turned away for a moment. "I realized that if he wasn't home, he had to be at his office," he said. "When I got there, he had you cornered. Your face was bruised; he had a broom handle in his hand…"

Turning back to her, he met her eyes. "I went a little crazy," he said. "I tackled him and started to hit him. I just couldn't stop. Thank God Sean arrived, or I might have killed him."

There was a brief moment of silence and Bradley wondered how Mary would react to his confession. He had been unprofessional. He had nearly killed a suspect.

Mary cocked her head to the side and bit her lower lip. "I'm afraid I'm going to shock you," she said. "But after living through what he did to Jeannine and knowing what he was going to do to me, I can't regret anything you did to him. You didn't hit him because you were angry; you hit him because you were avenging Jeannine. I know it's not the right way to view it, but thank you for making him be a victim, for at least a little while."

Tension he didn't realize he had been feeling was released. "I never want to be that out of control again," he said.

"I don't think that's something you have to worry about."

"How did you know the baby wasn't mine?" he asked. "You said something about hearing her cry before you passed out."

Mary took a deep breath and sat back in her pillows. "I was there, sort of, when Jeannine gave birth."

He shook his head. "I don't understand."

"You remember when I told you that Jeannine had to use my body in order to be hypnotized, right?"

He nodded.

"Well, it was more than just using my body," Mary explained. "I actually lived through all of her memories."

"Wait…so you experienced what Gary did to her?" he asked, the realization of her words staggering him. "You felt her fears? You felt… Did he rape you?"

Mary closed her eyes for a moment, took a deep breath and then faced Bradley. "Yes," she said, releasing the word with a shuddering exhale. "He raped her…me. Yes, I experienced everything he did to her."

"I should have killed him," Bradley said softly, his eyes hard with anger.

He stood up and walked away from her bed, facing the wall instead of looking into her eyes. Guilt and self-loathing filled him. He had asked for her help to solve Jeannine's murder. He had allowed her to be hypnotized. He was the reason she was lying in a hospital bed. He was the reason she was raped.

"Bradley?" Mary's shy, uncertain voice brought another wave of remorse.

"I am so sorry for what I've caused you," he rasped. "So damn sorry."

He heard her sigh deeply. "Bradley, you aren't going to be able to help me if you keep blaming yourself. And I really need your help."

"What?" he asked, spinning around to face her.

She was still sitting up at the top of the bed; the covers clasped in her hands and pulled up to her neck. Her face was pale and he could see that she was trying her hardest to be brave.

22

"I need your help," she said, her voice caught slightly, but she cleared her throat and continued. "I don't want him to win. I don't want to be afraid."

"What can I possibly do to help you, Mary?" he asked, lifting his hands in bewilderment. "I've let you down more than I've helped you lately. How do you know I won't make it worse?"

Taking a deep breath, she leaned forward and met his eyes. "Because you are the only man I've loved, Bradley Alden. And if you can't help me trust men again, then no one can."

He exhaled slowly and nodded. Keeping his eyes on hers, he walked back to the bed and sat down next to her. Leaning forward, he lifted his hand and lightly placed it against the side of her face, tenderly stroking her cheek with his thumb.

"He won't win, Mary," he said softly. "I'll help you."

He felt her stiffen under his hand, but he continued to rhythmically caress her.

"Besides, it would really be a shame," he said.

She took a deep breath; inhaling the familiar scent of him and trying to force herself to relax. "What would be a shame?"

"I bought one of those black spandex shirts you liked so much," he teased. "I'd hate to have to return it."

A giggle erupted from deep inside of her and her tension started to slip away.

"It took me hours to find the right one," he continued, moving his thumb so he gently grazed her lips. "I even called Ian and asked him where to shop."

"The right one?" she asked, her lips turning up in a smile.

"Aye," he said, trying to imitate Ian's accent. "One that will show off me man boobies."

Chuckling, she recalled their late night conversations over the Internet. She remembered his concern for her and his confidence in her. She studied his face for a moment and felt love replace her fear. She nestled her head into his hand, placing a soft kiss on his thumb. "I can't wait to see it," she said.

"I can't wait to show it to you," he said softly, gently sliding his thumb over her lips.

She stifled a yawn and smiled. "I guess I must be feeling more relaxed because suddenly I'm exhausted."

"Why don't you rest up for a bit? I'll stay here and watch over you."

"Thank you," she said, her eyelids slowly shutting. "I just need a nap, that's all."

"Sweet dreams, sweetheart," he whispered, slipping his hand out from under her head as her rhythmic breathing indicated she was already asleep. "We'll win. I promise."

# *Chapter Three*

A soft knock on the hospital room door an hour later immediately brought Bradley to full attention. He pushed himself out of the armchair he'd been resting in and positioned himself between Mary and the door.

Dr. Louise Thorne slipped into the room, her white lab coat over her blue jeans and flannel shirt. "How is she doing?" she asked in a low voice.

"Good. I guess," he replied.

"So what do you mean by that?"

He shrugged his shoulders. "Well, she was alert and didn't seem to have any memory loss or have any trouble speaking," he said. "But…"

He hesitated, trying to decide how much he could share with Dr. Thorne about Mary's experience. "She went through a fairly traumatic ordeal," he finally said. "It's hard to explain."

"Just tell me and I'll ask any questions," Dr. Thorne suggested.

"She was put under hypnosis to help solve a case and she actually lived through someone else's memories. She felt as though she was experiencing them – felt the pain and the emotion," he said. "This person, this victim, had been kidnapped, held for quite a few months and raped repeatedly."

Dr. Thorne took a deep breath and glanced over at Mary. "And she remembers it all?"

He nodded. "When she woke up…I was so relieved, so I hugged her," he said. "And she was afraid of me."

She put her hand on his arm. "Not you, Bradley," she said. "She is trying to deal with the psychological trauma. Fear is one of the most common and most understandable reactions when a woman is raped."

"Does she need counseling?"

Smiling, she looked over at Mary again. "Yes, that would be a good idea, but I have a feeling that Mary is the type who will try and tough it out on her own," she said. "Until she finally decides she needs help. You can't force her to get help, she has to decide it's a good idea."

"So, what do I do in the meantime?"

"What did she ask you to do?"

"She asked for my help," he said. "She wants to be able to trust again and she asked me to help her."

"That's sounds like a good start. If she is sleeping this soundly while you are in the room with her, she does trust you," she said. "And it seems that she understands this might be a long process. Bradley, have you had any experience with post-traumatic stress disorder?"

He nodded. "Yeah, some of the guys I served with had it."

"When a person is raped, they experience a disorder that is very similar," she explained. "They often have flashbacks or nightmares. They are more fearful than they used to be and often try to isolate themselves in order to feel some level of security. The world is not a safe place for them anymore."

Bradley's jaw tightened. He turned away from Dr. Thorne and his gaze rested on Mary.

"Did you rape her?" Dr. Thorne asked sharply.

Bradley turned back quickly. "What? Hell no," he whispered fiercely.

Dr. Thorne nodded and stepped up to face Bradley. "Then stop clenching your jaw and letting your anger get the best of you," she said. "Yes, whoever did this deserves the worst punishment available. But that's not going to help Mary. What's going to help her is you being calm and supportive. Do you understand?"

He took a deep breath and nodded. "Yeah, I got it Doc."

"You got it, but can you do it?" she asked, her eyebrows raised.

He nodded. "Yeah, I will do it."

"Good, now let's get her checked out of this hospital and home as soon as we can," she said.

Shaking his head, Bradley wondered if he heard her correctly. "Home?" he asked. "Doesn't she need to be in the hospital?"

Moving to the bed and scanning the clipboard at the end, she nodded. "Oh, if it were anyone else, they'd be staying," she said. "But being here adds more stress than benefits. And I know that between you and the rest of your tight-knit group, she'll be well watched over. Although, I need you to promise me if you see anything that concerns you, you'll call me immediately."

"Yes, I promise," he agreed. "And you're right, she will be well looked after."

Dr. Thorne grinned. "Yes, I thought so. Why don't you go down the hall and get something to drink while Mary and I have a conversation."

She put the clipboard down and moved along the side of the bed. "Mary," she said, "Mary, I need you to wake up so I can examine you."

Mary mumbled in her sleep and nestled further into her pillow. "Mary, I really need you to wake up," Dr. Thorne said in a firmer and louder voice.

Mary's eyes sprang open and she turned quickly. "Oh, Dr. Thorne, I'm so sorry, I didn't hear you come in."

Then she saw him, the translucent ghost standing behind Dr. Thorne. But he wasn't trying to get Mary's attention; he was just watching Dr. Thorne.

"Mary, Mary," Dr. Thorne repeated. "Now, how are you feeling?"

Mary shook her head. "Sorry. I'm better, much better," she quickly answered. "I really don't think I need to stay here any longer."

The ghost moved closer, but the sunlight streaming through the window onto his face blurred his features.

Cocking her head, Dr. Thorne took Mary's wrist in her hand and checked her pulse. "And why don't you think you need to stay here?" she asked.

"Well," Mary paused for a moment and then brightened. "I actually have a doctor staying with me. Right in my home."

Dr. Thorne looked over her shoulder at Bradley. "You never mentioned that," she said.

He cleared his throat. "I guess I didn't think of Ian in that way," he responded, earning a grateful smile from Mary.

Giving Mary a speculative look, she pulled the cloth screen around the bed, separating them from Bradley. She pulled her stethoscope from around her neck and put it on. She bent over and placed the end against Mary's chest. "Okay, Mary, take a deep breath," she said.

Mary complied and Dr. Thorne moved the stethoscope to the left. "So, what kind of doctor is Ian?" she asked.

Mary coughed and Dr. Thorne lifted the stethoscope. "I didn't need you to cough, Mary," she said. "And although I know you've stretched the truth from time to time, I've never known you to lie to me."

Mary sighed. "He's a Ph.D.," she said. "I don't think he even knows how to take someone's temperature."

Dr. Thorne laughed. "Well, good, a Ph.D. is just the kind of person you need to look after you. I'm releasing you immediately, provided you take it easy and call me if there are any things that concern you."

Shocked, Mary sat up, open-mouthed and stared at the doctor for a moment. "Really? I can just go home?"

Moving closer, Dr. Thorne perched on the edge of the bed. "Mary, you can go home and relax," she said. "But you need to remember sometimes you can't handle things all by yourself. Sometimes the only way to solve a problem is by bringing an expert in to help you."

"Bradley told you?" she asked.

Nodding, Dr. Thorne met Mary's gaze. "You are a strong woman," she said. "But you are also smart and I hope you realize there is nothing wrong with going to someone to talk about your feelings and your fears."

"Yes," Mary responded. "I know and I'm not afraid to seek help if I need it."

Dr. Thorne smiled. "And if others suggest highly that you might need it," she said. "You might want to consider they may have a better perspective than you."

"Understood," she agreed.

"Good!" the doctor said, standing. "Now I'll pull Bradley out of here so you can get dressed. I'll have the nurse back in here with your discharge papers in the next twenty minutes or so."

The ghost was still there and Mary knew there had to be a connection between the ghost and her doctor. "Dr. Thorne," Mary said, before the doctor pulled the curtain aside. "Why did you become a doctor? Was your father a doctor?"

She shook her head. "No, my father was actually a chemistry teacher at the high school. He died in an explosion at the high school when I was a little girl."

"Oh, I'm so sorry."

"I regret not knowing who he really was," she said. "I missed not having a father."

"Well, I'm sure he'd be proud of who you are," Mary said.

"Thank you, Mary."

# Chapter Four

"I can't believe you tried to lie to Dr. Thorne," Bradley said, chuckling, as he helped Mary up the stairs of her home.

"I didn't lie to her," Mary replied, punching in the code for the lock. "I just didn't explain in great detail."

"You told her you had a doctor living with you," Bradley clarified, opening the door and following Mary into the house.

She turned back and placed her hands on her hips. "Well, Ian's a Ph.D., so he's a doctor."

"So, Mary, me darling, are you asking me to play doctor with you?"

"No, she's not," Bradley said firmly. "But you do get to help play nursemaid."

"I don't need a nursemaid," she insisted. "Or a bevy of them for that matter."

She leaned against the wall, surprised at how exhausted she was just from the trip home.

"How are you feeling, there?" Ian asked, leaning forward and placing a kiss on her cheek.

She smiled up at him. "I'm good," she said. "It's good to be home."

"Would you like some lunch?" he asked. "I'm making haggis." He wiggled his eyebrows at her.

32

"Well, darn it. I ate at the hospital before I came home," she said with a sigh. "And I so wanted to try haggis."

"Well, I made plenty," he teased. "Day old haggis for breakfast." He rubbed his stomach. "Yum."

She laughed and turned to Bradley. "You can take me back to the hospital now," she jested. "Ian has finally found a way to keep me there."

"No way, we have you here and now we're in charge," Bradley said, pushing the door behind him.

A gust of wind caught the door and it slammed against the frame. Mary paled and pushed herself against the wall, her breath catching in her throat.

"Darling, what's wrong?" Ian asked, moving toward her.

"No," she cried out, raising her hands to ward him off. "Please don't come closer."

"Damn it," Bradley said softly. "I'm sorry, Mary. That was a stupid thing to do."

She turned to him, her eyes wide and frightened. "He slammed the door," she whispered. "When he came to see me, to hurt me, he slammed the door."

"It wasn't him; the wind just caught the door, that's all. You're safe now," he said calmly. "You're safe and Ian and I will protect you. He can't hurt you ever again."

She nodded and took a deep breath, sinking against the wall. "I'm sorry, Ian," she whispered, placing her hand on his shoulder. "Just a bad reaction."

Bradley scooped her up into his arms. "Come on, Mary. I think you've had enough excitement for today. Ian, help me get her up to her room."

"I'm fine," she whispered weakly against his chest.

"Aye, he knows you're fine," Ian teased softly, gathering her things and following Bradley up the stairs. "He just has to show off his muscles every once in a while to keep you impressed."

She chuckled softly. "Well, I am impressed."

Bradley held her tighter and placed a kiss on the top of her head. "Good, it worked."

The three made their way to her room. Ian pulled her covers back and Bradley placed her gently on the bed. Ian leaned back behind her and plumped up the pillows and Bradley tucked the blankets around her.

Then the two men stepped back and looked down at her.

"I think she needs a wee dram of tea," Ian said to Bradley, "with a touch of honey in it."

Bradley nodded. "And toast," he added. "She needs toast and...scrambled eggs."

"Aye, scrambled eggs, the very thing," Ian agreed. "You know how to make them, don't you?"

"Can't be that hard," Bradley reasoned. "Crack some eggs together and fry them in butter."

"I'm not very hungry," Mary inserted.

"I think you add some cream to the eggs," Ian said, ignoring Mary's comment. "And then you add salt and pepper."

"That's right," Bradley said. "And we could put jam on her toast."

"Aye, or marmalade," Ian added. "Orange marmalade is the cure for most anything that ails you."

"Really," Mary tried again, "I'm not hungry."

"Well, fine, I'll start the kettle," Ian said, walking to the door.

"Great, I know where she keeps her frying pan," Bradley said, joining him.

The door closed behind them. Mary sat in the bed, shaking her head, a smile spreading across her face. *With nursemaids like those two, I won't have to worry about anything.*

Her gaze moved to the other door across the room. The bathroom. She would give anything for a shower. She lifted her arm and sniffed. *Oh, gross!!! A shower was a definite necessity.*

She pushed the blankets off, slipped to the edge of the bed and placed her feet on the floor. Taking her time, she stood and assessed her strength. *I feel good,* she told herself. *I feel good enough to march across this room and take a shower.*

She ventured to her dresser and pulled out clean undergarments and her loungewear of choice, Chicago Police Department sweats. Then she carefully walked across the room to the tiled bathroom.

She leaned into the shower and adjusted the multiple shower heads and the temperature of the water. Turning the water on to heat, she pulled a large fluffy bath towel from the shelf and hung it on the hook next to the shower door. Reaching in, she let the water run over her hand and smiled at the perfect temperature.

After slipping out of her clothes and dropping them in the hamper, she stepped into the shower. She closed her eyes in pure bliss as the hot water sluiced over her skin and massaged her sore muscles with pulsating sprays. Reaching up to the shelf that held her bath products, she grabbed her body wash, poured a generous amount onto her sponge and inhaled the refreshing citrus scent. Turning in the shower, she began to reach for her shampoo and froze in her tracks. As steam filled the small enclosure and fogged up the glass, words started to appear on the door of the shower as if written by an invisible hand. "Here's looking at you, kid."

Mary screamed and jumped back, knocking into the wall and causing her bath products to come crashing down on the shower floor. She grabbed the towel, quickly wrapped it around her wet and soapy body and began to step out of the shower just as the final two words appeared. "Love, Mike."

"Mike!" Mary yelled, as she stormed wet and dripping from the bathroom. "Mike, I know you can hear me!"

She ignored the thundering of two sets of male feet up the stairs and stood in the center of her room, hands on her hips. "I know you're there!"

"Mary! Are you okay?" Bradley yelled as he and Ian burst into the room.

"Mike! Answer me!"

"Did the doctor say anything about strange behavior?" Ian whispered to Bradley.

Mary turned and glared at Ian.

"Sorry," he said, ducking behind Bradley.

"Mary, what's wrong?" Bradley asked.

"Mike," she called out again, ignoring Bradley. "Get your dead butt down here."

"Nice outfit, Mary," Mike said when he appeared in the middle of the room. He looked around. "What? Are we having a party?"

Mary tucked in the edge of her towel for a tighter grip. "The rule was no entering my bathroom," she said. "You broke the rule."

"What?" he asked, then realization hit. "Oh, crap, I forgot about my note."

"Yeah, well, I really didn't appreciate the surprise," she said, her voice cracking.

"Oh, Mary, I'm so sorry," he said, moving closer. "It was just meant to be a joke."

"Well, it wasn't funny," Mary said, wiping the water from her brow. "At least, it wasn't funny today."

"What did he do?" Bradley asked, moving toward the shower.

"You can see him?" Mary and Ian asked simultaneously.

Bradley fished in his pocket and pulled out the glass stone Mike had given him. "Yeah, he let me use the magic stone Ian gave you, so I could see him," Bradley explained.

"I didn't give Mary a stone," Ian said, "magic or otherwise."

Bradley looked across the room to the vase filled with similar stones and then turned to Mike. "Magic stones?"

Mike grinned. "You had the ability in you all the time, you just needed a little confidence in yourself," he said. "And obviously, it worked."

"You thought my glass beads were magic?" she chuckled.

She looked over at the vase on her dresser, but then caught their reflection in the mirror. Her hair was wet and dripping, her skin was still covered in lather and her bath towel reached only about half-way down her thighs. She moved one hand and adjusted the towel's edge behind her, just to be sure nothing was hanging out. The other hand clasped the towel edge that was tucked into the middle of her chest. She felt the blush start at her face and move down to her toes.

"Okay, well, everything's fine," she said. "You can all leave now."

"Are you sure you don't need…?" Ian began.

"Very sure, thanks," Mary interrupted, walking backwards to the bathroom.

"I could help…" Bradley offered.

"Oh, no," she interrupted again. "I'm good."

They still stood there, not moving, concern on their faces. *This calls for drastic action*, she thought.

"Do I smell eggs and toast burning?" she asked, sniffing the air.

"Oh, the toast," Ian said, rushing from the room.

"I thought I turned those eggs off," Bradley yelled as he hurried down the stairs.

Mike grinned at her. "Good job," he said, and then his grin disappeared and his face grew thoughtful. "I am sorry. You know I would never do anything to upset you."

She nodded. "Yes, I do," she acknowledged with a smile. "Now get out of my bedroom and stay the hell out of my bathroom, please."

"Yes, ma'am," he chuckled, and then faded away.

# Chapter Five

"So, how is she really doing?" Ian asked Bradley, as they waited for Mary to finish her shower.

Bradley shook his head. "Well, physically she's fine, a little weak, but good. However, Dr. Thorne wants us to keep an eye on her and make sure she doesn't sleep for too long."

"And the not-physically part?" Ian asked.

Sighing, Bradley sat down in a chair next to the kitchen table and put his head in his hands. "She's suffering a kind of post-traumatic stress from Jeannine's memories and from her own kidnapping."

"Ahhh, well that explains the episode near the door," Ian said, leaning over the kitchen counter. "So, what can we do to help her?"

Bradley looked up at Ian and shook his head. "It's got to come from her," he said. "We can be patient and supportive, but she has to decide when and if she'll go and get help."

"Psychiatric help you mean," Ian said.

Nodding, Bradley sat back in the chair. "Yes," he replied. "But she doesn't know how she can explain what happened to her, to a psychiatrist."

"Aye, I can see that'd be a problem."

"She was hoping that you could hypnotize her again and remove some of Jeannine's memories."

"The rub there is that hypnosis is based in suggestion and trust," Ian explained. "She'd have to trust me enough to allow me to bring her under again. I don't know if she'd be ready for that just now."

"We'll just have to help her be ready," Bradley stated. "I just…"

"You just wish you could fix everything for her and protect her while you were doing it," he said.

Bradley nodded. "Yeah, how did you know?"

"Well, that's exactly what my dear Gillian says we men try to do all the time," he said with a chuckle. "And damn if she's not always right."

Their conversation ended when they heard the door to Mary's room open and heard her walking down the hall.

"Should we help her down the stairs?" Ian asked.

Bradley shook his head. "No, but being close in case she needs help isn't a bad idea," he decided. "We should make it look like we're not waiting to help her though."

They both moved to the bottom of the staircase. Ian looked around quickly and then nodded his head. "Aye, I can see that spot above the cabinets," he said loudly. "You're right; it could be a water leak. Though it could also just be a shadow."

Bradley sent Ian a grateful smile. "Yes, that's what I thought too. The only way to check it is to pull out the ladder and get up there."

Mary paused, looked down at the two men and grinned. The ceiling above the cabinets was

41

pristine and white; there were no shadows or marks. She knew they were there to be sure she didn't need any help, and she appreciated it. She continued her slow descent, stopping on the step above the kitchen floor to join in on their conversation.

"Do you think it will be costly to repair?" she asked.

"Oh, Mary, you're here," Ian said, as he offered her his hand and helped her down the last step. "How are you feeling, love?"

She smiled. "Better, much better, thank you."

Bradley pulled a chair away from the kitchen table and helped her sit down. "Right after you eat, we'll get you situated on the couch," he said. "Ian already has a fire started in the fireplace."

"That would be lovely, thank you," she smiled up at Bradley and pressed a kiss on his cheek.

"Well, if you're passing out kisses…" Ian bent down and offered his cheek.

Laughing, Mary pressed a soft kiss on his cheek too. "Thank you, Ian."

Bradley placed a plate filled with scrambled eggs and toast in front of her. The eggs were piled several inches high and the toast was thickly slathered with butter and jam.

"Um, how many eggs did you scramble?" she asked.

"I think it was four, no maybe six," he said, with an apologetic shrug. "Ian and I were talking and I got a little distracted."

"Why don't you and Ian sit down and help me eat some of this," she suggested. "I generally don't eat a half dozen eggs and six pieces of toast for breakfast."

"Are you sure?" Ian asked, pulling a couple of plates from the cabinet.

She nodded. "Oh, yes, I'm completely sure."

The meal was accomplished without incident with the two men doing their best to make Mary laugh. They had both just settled Mary into the recliner, complete with a pillow for her back, fleece blanket for her feet and a cup of tea at her side, when the doorbell rang. Before anyone could answer, Stanley let himself in, followed closely by a disapproving Rosie.

"Stanley, you just don't walk into someone's home," Rosie said, turning to Stanley and not acknowledging anyone else in the room.

"It ain't just anyone's home, it's Mary's," he argued.

"But it's not polite," she replied.

"I rang the bell first," he said. "So iffen she was doing something she didn't want us to see, she had a chance to stop."

Mary chuckled. "Please come in, I insist."

Stanley nodded his head smugly. "See, she insists."

Rosie sniffed. "Well, of course she did, she's polite."

Both of the sassy senior citizens had become Mary's best friends during the few years she had lived in Freeport. Stanley was the fifth generation owner of Wagner's Office Products and Rosie was a successful real estate broker in Freeport. They had not only become an essential part of Mary's life and her private investigation team, they had also fallen in love with each other.

The two slipped off their coats and laid them on the back of a chair before crossing the room to where Mary reclined on the couch. Rosie sat on the chair adjacent to her and Stanley perched on the chair's arm.

"How are you doing?" Rosie asked, leaning forward and placing her hand on Mary's arm.

Mary covered Rosie's hand with her own. "I'm good," she said. "And I have two of the best nursemaids in Freeport looking out for me."

"He ain't trying to make you eat any foreign food, is he?" Stanley asked, sending a distrustful glance at Ian.

"Oh, aye, I've been trying to force haggis and blood pudding down her throat," Ian said. "But this big brute of a policeman won't let me."

"Humph, he ain't much better," Stanley grumbled looking over at Bradley. "But at least he's got some common sense and can speak English."

"Thank you, Stanley," Bradley said. "Coming from you, I feel extremely complimented."

Stanley made his way over to Mary and crouched down next to the recliner. "It's about time you decided to stop loafing around at the hospital and get back to the real world," he said. "Some of us have important things to talk to you about."

"Oh, and what would that be?" Mary asked, lifting her eyebrows.

Stanley blushed and shrugged his shoulders. "You tell her, Rosie," he mumbled. "This here's womanly talk anyhow."

Rosie leaned over and kissed Stanley on the cheek. "Isn't he the sweetest thing?" she asked Mary.

"Dang it, woman, you can't do that kind of stuff in public," he stammered, getting up and walking across the room.

"But Stanley, this isn't public, this is Mary's house," Rosie replied with a smile.

She turned back to Mary. "Mary, Stanley and I are engaged!"

Mary's jaw dropped with surprise. Her dearest friends, who constantly bickered at each other, finally realized how much they were in love. She felt tears well up in her eyes. "I am so happy for you," she sniffed. "This is just so wonderful."

"Yeah, if it's so wonderful, why are you bawling your eyes out?" Stanley asked.

"Come here, you old curmudgeon and give me a hug," she demanded.

Stanley, his face slightly pink and his grin stretched from ear to ear, walked over and gave Mary a soft hug. "Congratulations," she whispered in his ear. "She's a lucky lady."

He shook his head. "Naw, I'm the lucky one."

Stanley moved back and Rosie scooted forward. "I know you're still recovering, but I have to know," Rosie exclaimed. "Mary, would you be my maid-of-honor?"

"Oh, I would be delighted," she said.

"Well, good," Stanley grumbled. "Cause I 'spect there ain't many women in this town who'd be able to work with my best man."

He nodded over in Bradley's direction. "I asked him at the hospital the other day."

Mary turned to Bradley. "You knew and you didn't tell me?"

He shrugged. "I guess my mind was on other things."

"When's the wedding?" Mary asked.

"Saint Patrick's Day," Rosie said. "Stanley insisted because his memory is so bad he knew he'd forget our anniversary if we didn't have it on a holiday."

"Well, Valentine's Day is only a couple of weeks away," Mary teased.

"Aw, everyone gets married on Valentine's," Stanley said. "We wanted ours to be unique."

"No matter what, I'm sure your wedding is going to be unique," Ian said. "It's not often a beauty marries a beast."

Stanley chuckled. "You've got that right," he said. "That's why I picked St. Pat's because I knew I was the luckiest man on earth."

"Oh, Stanley," Rosie cooed, "that was so romantic."

Stanley blushed. "Well, it's just the truth, that's all."

Rosie walked over to Stanley and put her arms around his neck. "I think we are going to have to leave now because I want to kiss you and I know you don't want all of these people to see it."

"Just don't want them to be jealous, that's all," he mumbled. "'Sides, Mary is recovering, so we ought to let her get her rest."

"Oh, aye, that's one of the best excuses I've ever heard," Ian said with a grin. "And I almost believe it. How about you Bradley?"

"If I get a report that you two are parked somewhere steaming up the windows, I'm not going to be too happy about it."

Rosie giggled. "We'll make sure to wipe the windows clear every so often."

Bradley laughed. "Good enough," he said. "Now get out of here before you make us all tired."

# Chapter Six

"I'm tired," Mary said, shifting in the recliner. "You two wouldn't mind if I went upstairs to bed, would you?"

Bradley and Ian looked up from the movie on the television in amazement. "But Mary, they haven't solved the murder yet," Ian said.

She shrugged. "I have. Do you want to know who did it?"

Ian clapped his hands over his ears. "No, don't tell me."

Bradley chuckled and rose to his feet. "Come on, Sherlock, I'll walk you upstairs. Ian why don't you make us some popcorn and we less than brilliant viewers can finish the rest of the movie."

"I didn't say you weren't brilliant," Mary protested. "I just solved the mystery. I worked on a case like this in Chicago. You see, the spouse..."

Ian pressed his hands tighter over his ears. "La, la, la, la, la," he sang. "I can't hear you."

"What the hell is he doing? A Scottish mating dance?" Mike asked, appearing in the middle of the room.

"Yeah, don't get too close," Bradley said.

"Oh, very funny, Bradley," Ian said, getting up from his chair. "Go put Mary to bed; Mike can keep me company until you return."

"Oh, cool, I love this movie," Mike said, "especially the end when we find out the butler did it."

"AHHHHHHHHH!" Ian screamed, running into the kitchen.

Mike looked at Ian and then turned to Mary and Bradley. "What? What just happened here?"

Mary and Bradley turned to each other and started to laugh.

"What?" Mike asked.

Mary collapsed against Bradley, tears running down her cheeks. "I can't breathe," she gasped as she laughed. "My sides ache."

Bradley wrapped an arm around her and led her to the staircase, his own laughter echoing in the room. "Come on; let's escape while we still have brain cells left."

"What?" Mike called again, confusion evident in his voice.

"Oh shut up," Ian yelled from the kitchen. "And pick something else to watch on the bloody telly."

A fresh wave of laughter floated down the stairs from Mary and Bradley.

"It's not that funny," Ian called up after them.

Bradley and Mary sat on the edge of her bed, wiping the tears from their eyes. Mary took a deep breath. "Oh, that felt so good," she said breathlessly. "I really needed that."

He turned and wiped a stray tear from her cheek and she smiled up at him. "It feels like it's been forever since we laughed together."

He smiled and nodded. "I agree."

Looking up at him, she gave him a cheeky grin. "It feels like forever since we did several things together, Police Chief Alden."

"Like what?"

She looped her arms around his shoulders. "Like this," she whispered, before kissing him lightly on the lips.

Loosely encircling her waist with his arms, he pulled her a little closer. "Yeah, I missed that too."

"Me too," she replied with a sigh. "I missed you."

"Never again," he said, lowering his head to touch her forehead. "Never again will I let doubt and fears keep us apart."

She sighed happily. "So what should I promise?"

"Promise to love me forever," he whispered, kissing her lightly on the nose.

"Oh, well, that's easy," she replied, lifting her head to kiss his lips.

He angled his head and deepened the kiss, pouring all of his love into it. She slid her arms tighter around his neck, knocking them both off-balance. They slipped backwards onto the bed, Mary still enfolded in his arms.

She froze. Suddenly she was back in the dark room and Gary was climbing on her, touching her.

"No, no," she cried, beating against his chest. "Don't touch me, don't touch me."

"Mary! Mary, it's me," Bradley insisted, lifting himself away from her. "I'm so sorry. Mary, come back to me."

She scrambled across the bed until she was in the far corner. Her eyes were wide and frightened, her breath coming out in gasps. Bradley could tell she wasn't seeing her own bedroom, she was back with Gary.

"Mary, you're home," he said softly. "You're in your own room. No one will hurt you. Mary, you're safe. I promise. You're safe."

The glaze of fear left her eyes and she blinked several times. She looked around her room and then looked at Bradley. He was standing a few feet from the bed looking down at her with concern on his face. "Bradley?" she whispered.

"Mary?" he said in a low voice. "Are you okay? Do you know where you are?"

She nodded, tears running unchecked down her face. "Oh, Bradley, am I going crazy?"

He slowly moved toward the bed, and when she didn't object, climbed over next to her. He wrapped his arms around her and held her as she cried, kissing her on the top of her head. "No, darling, you're not crazy. We've just got to give you a little more time to heal."

# Chapter Seven

Once he had assured himself she was doing better, Bradley left Mary's room, closing the door firmly behind him. Ian stood at the top of the staircase and Mike hovered nearby.

"We heard something and thought we'd come and have a look," Ian said.

"No, we thought we'd have to kick your ass if you were hurting her," Mike corrected, and then he looked at the worry on Bradley's face. "Not that we actually thought you'd be hurting her."

Bradley sat on the top step and put his head in his hands. "One moment, everything's fine, everything's great and the next moment, she thinks I'm Gary."

Ian placed his hand on Bradley's shoulder. "Oh, no, she doesn't think you're Gary," he said. "She's having a flashback. She's not home anymore; her mind brought her back to Jeannine's memories. It's naught to do with you."

Scoffing harshly, Bradley shook his head. "Yeah, you try to convince yourself of that when she's beating her hands against your chest and screaming in terror."

"So, you've never had a woman do that to you before?" Mike teased.

"It's not funny, Mike," Bradley replied, but he couldn't help the smile that flitted over his face.

"No, it's not funny," he said. "But you have to get some perspective here. Mary is safe. Gary is going to be put away for a long time. But, even if he escaped, Mary could have kicked his butt with no problem, as long as she wasn't drugged. She's not a victim. She's a warrior. She just has to remember."

Ian nodded. "Pretty smart for a dead guy."

Turning to Ian, Mike grinned. "Yeah, and I don't even have a Ph.D."

They walked down the stairs together and gathered at the kitchen table where Ian had placed a large bowl of buttered popcorn and some drinks.

"I figured since there was no point in watching the rest of the movie, we might want to decide how we can best help Mary," he said.

"Well…" Bradley began.

"Shouldn't I be included in the conversation?"

The three turned to see Mary standing on the staircase, wrapped in her robe and looking determined.

"Aye, you should," Ian agreed. "Have a seat and I'll get you something to drink? Would you like tea?"

She shook her head. "No, I need something stronger. Is there any cold Diet Pepsi?"

Mike grinned. "The champ is back and she's fighting."

Mary shook her head as she came down the stairs and joined the men. "No, I'm not fighting, I'm scared. But I know I can't go on like this. So, any suggestions?"

Ian handed Mary a can of soda and sat down next to her. "Let me hypnotize you," he said. "I might be able to remove Jeannine's memories. You'd still have your abduction to deal with, but I think it would lessen the trauma."

Shaking her head, she took a deep breath. "Can we take that off the table for now?" she asked. "I don't think I want to be hypnotized again for a while."

Ian stiffened, taken aback. "I'm sorry, Mary," he said, his voice strained. "I had no idea it would have this effect on you. I never…"

She quickly turned to him and placed her hand on his shoulder. "That's not what I meant," she said. "We both did what we needed to do to solve this crime and I don't regret it for a moment. Please don't think I hold you responsible for any of this."

"But…" he began, but stopped when he saw the plea for understanding in her eyes.

Cocking his head to the side, he studied her for a moment. "I see," he said slowly, staring into her eyes. "I agree we should pursue some other options."

"After 9/11 we got a lot of training about post-traumatic stress disorder," Mike said. "Lots of the first responders were affected."

Mouthing a silent "thank you" to Ian, Mary turned to Mike. "What kinds of things were suggested?"

"Talk to someone about your experience," Bradley interjected.

"Well, there aren't too many professionals who would listen to my story without suggesting I go to a nice quiet place and rest for a long time," she replied wryly.

"It doesn't have to be a psychologist," Mike said. "You can talk to us. Get it out of your system."

She looked at the three strong, capable and caring men sitting at the table. She knew they'd listen and do their best to empathize with her. But they would never really be able to understand what she experienced.

"As much as I appreciate it, I don't think…" she tried to explained. "What happened to me…to Jeannine…"

"We aren't women and we can't understand how it feels to be raped," Ian stated baldly.

"Yes," she said softly. "That's it exactly."

"Well, what else?" he asked.

"You've got to get busy," Mike said. "You've got to get back to living your life. Don't let the experience rule your life."

"Hey, she just got out of the hospital," Bradley protested. "She needs some down time."

"I wasn't suggesting she run a marathon," Mike said. "Just start moving forward."

"An investigation," Ian said, "an old case with a calm, easy-going ghost. Something I can use for one of my studies."

"Perfect!" Mary said. "And I have just the case. While I was at the hospital there was a ghost following Dr. Thorne. Then she told me her father died in an explosion at the high school. We could look into that one."

"Wait," Bradley interrupted. "I think you are all moving too fast."

She turned to him and placed her hand over his. "I promise I won't over-do," she said. "I just have to get busy, get my mind off of what happened."

He turned his hand and caught her hand in his own. "Not thinking about it is not going to make it go away," he said. "I could speak with Regina Tallmadge at VOICES, the domestic violence shelter; she could get you into a group session."

She knew Bradley meant well and was only trying to protect her, but she wasn't like those other women. She was a trained professional. She understood about crimes against women. She wasn't a victim. She had been a cop. A damned good cop. And if she could survive dying, there was no way in hell some creep was going to get the best of her.

She squeezed his hand and met his eyes. "I'm not ready for that," she said. "But I'll be sure to let you know as soon as I am."

"Yeah, Mary doesn't need to sit around talking, she needs some action and she needs it now," Mike said.

There was a sharp rap on the front door, causing everyone to jump.

"Okay, that was spooky," Mike added.

# Chapter Eight

The men allowed Mary to open her own door, but only after earning a sharp glare when they tried to prevent her. "It's my house," she said with determination. "I can answer the door."

She was surprised to find Andy's mom, Katie Brennan, standing on the porch. In the past few months, Katie and Mary had become good friends. Katie was wrapped in a camel-colored coat with a soft pink and lavender wool scarf layered around her neck. Her curly blond hair poked out in wisps from the matching knitted cap and her usually sparkling blue eyes were filled with concern. She hadn't been outside for very long, because her cheeks hadn't reddened enough to cover the smattering of freckles across her cheeks. Mary knew she was the mother of six, but at this moment she could have been mistaken for a college coed.

"Mary, I have a huge favor to ask you," she said, concern audible in her voice.

"Is everything okay?" Mary asked. "Is Andy...?"

Katie smiled warmly. "No, everything's fine with the children, thanks for worrying. But the favor has to do with Andy and Maggie."

"Well, please, come in and tell me what you need," Mary insisted.

"I hate to be a bother," Katie replied.

"No, bother," Mary said, guiding her into the house. "Can I get you some tea?"

Katie stopped when she saw the two men standing in the living room. "Oh, Ian and Bradley, I'm so sorry, I didn't mean to interrupt," she exclaimed.

"Katie you're looking as pretty as a summer's day," Ian said. "Come in, we can make ourselves scarce if need be."

"No, please don't," she said. "I'm asking Mary a favor, but I'm afraid it's probably going to affect the two of you."

"What do you need?" Bradley asked.

Katie took a deep breath. "We just got a call that Clifford's mother, Andy's grandmother, took a fall at the nursing home she's been living in," she explained. "They believe she's broken her hip and they are taking her in to surgery tomorrow. She's fairly frail and we're concerned…"

Her voice cracked and she took a deep breath. "Well, we just don't want her to be alone right now."

"Of course not," Mary said. "How can I help?"

"I've found a place for the older boys to stay," she said. "But I need somewhere for Andy and Maggie to stay for at least a few days, and perhaps up to a week. I know they adore you and since the bus picks them up right in front of your house, I wondered…"

Mary smiled brightly. "Really?" she said, delighted. "You'd let me watch them for you?"

A shaky laugh burbled from Katie. "You obviously have no idea what you are getting yourself into," she said. "But if they are with you, I know I wouldn't have to worry about them at all."

"Would it be better if Ian and I limited our time at Mary's?" Bradley asked. "I don't want them to feel uncomfortable."

Katie laughed and shook her head. "You've become one of his heroes," she replied. "If there were a Police Chief Alden action figure, I believe you would have even replaced Wolverine."

"Big tall beast-like creature," Mike whispered to those who could see him. "Yeah, I can see the resemblance."

"And I do believe my Maggie has a crush on Ian," she said.

He chuckled. "Aye, she's a rare bonnie lassie," he said. "She'll be breaking hearts when she's older."

"Needless to say, I'd love to have them stay here," Mary said. "And I promise to take good care of them."

Katie shook her head. "I'm not worried about that. I'm worried about how much you're going to spoil them while I'm away."

Laughing, Mary shrugged her shoulders. "Well, you might have a little to worry on that count. But I'll try not to spoil them too much. When do you want to bring them over?"

Hesitating for a moment, Katie said, "Well, if it isn't too much of an imposition, I could bring them over now. We have to leave for the airport in the next couple of hours."

"Now would be great," Mary said. "Is there anything they shouldn't eat? Anyone I should call if they get sick?"

"They'll eat you out of house and home," Katie said. "And don't let them talk you into a diet of sweets and snacks."

"Ach, no, they'll have porridge for breakfast to get a good start of the day," Ian said. "I'm sure the wee kiddies would enjoy that. And would you like us to prepare a lunch for them to bring to school? I could whip up some meat pies…"

"They usually bring a lunch from home, but they can eat lunch at school if you'd rather not," Katie said. "And I'll bring over a list of emergency numbers and a letter giving you medical power of attorney in case there's an emergency and you can't get in touch with us."

"I'm sure everything will be fine," Bradley said. "Mary is not only great with the kids; she was also trained as an emergency responder through the Chicago Police Department. She's probably better trained than most EMTs."

Katie released a slow breath. "I didn't know that," she said. "And, I have to say, it eases my mind even more."

"I'll get the other guest room ready," Mary said. "It has a full sized bed and a trundle bed too. Will that work?"

"Oh, yes, that will be perfect," she said. "I know that Andy is going to be fine, but Maggie is a little nervous when she's away from home. Being close to her brother will help quite a bit. Thank you, Mary. I can't tell you how much this means to me."

"No need to thank me," Mary said. "I was just looking for something to keep me occupied for a little while. This is a heaven-sent blessing."

Katie walked to the door and let herself out. "Well, hopefully by the end of the week, you'll still think they were sent from heaven rather than somewhere else."

# Chapter Nine

Ten-year-old Andy Brennan and his eight-year-old sister, Maggie, were almost as thrilled as Mary when they arrived at her home less than fifteen minutes later.

"Guess what Mary?" Andy said, his eyes sparkling with pleasure. "I get to stay at your house for…"

He glanced over to his mother for confirmation.

"A few days," Katie said.

He nodded. "A few days…or maybe a week…or maybe even a year."

"I know," Mary said. "I'm pretty excited about it."

"Is he staying here too?" Maggie asked, pointing shyly at Ian.

Squatting down next to her, Ian winked at her. "Aye, I'm staying here too," he said. "Is that fine with you, or would you be throwing me out in the street this cold winter night?"

She giggled and pressed herself against her mother's leg. "He's the one," she whispered to her mother.

Katie's eyes grew round with understanding and then she nodded and grinned. "Well, of course, that makes perfect sense," she said. "Did you want to tell him or shall we keep it a secret?"

Maggie peeked out from behind the shelter of her mother and smiled at Ian. "I'm going to marry you when I grow up."

Pressing a hand to his heart, Ian smiled softly at her. "Well, now, that's the nicest thing someone's said to me in a long time. I suppose I should visit with your father, just to ask his permission before we get married."

Maggie nodded. "Yes, that's the way polite gentlemens do it."

"Aye, that's exactly right," Ian replied. "I suppose we should wait until you're at least twelve or so. What do you think?"

Sighing, Maggie shook her head. "My daddy says I can't date until I'm twenty-four. That's pretty far away."

Ian grinned. "Well, I don't blame your da in the least," he agreed. "If you were my daughter, I'd make you wait until you were thirty."

Katie placed a light hand on Maggie's head and gently stroked her hair. "Maggie's father is a little protective of his only daughter," Katie said with a smile. "Although with so many big brothers, I don't think he has much to worry about."

"My brothers were the main reason I didn't date much in high school," Mary said. "The other boys were too afraid of the wrath of the O'Reillys."

Bradley grinned and placed his arm around Mary's shoulders. "Another reason I'm grateful she has big brothers."

Katie looked up and laughed. "Ah, I see how it is," she said. "How long have you two been dating?"

Mary thought for a moment and then shook her head slightly. "Well, actually, Bradley and I have never gone on an actual date."

Looking down at her, Bradley shook his head. "That can't be right," he said. "What about…?"

He thought for a moment and finally sighed. "Well, da…I mean, darn, you're right. We've never had an actual date."

"Gentlemens take girls on dates," Maggie said.

Bradley grinned down at Maggie. "You are absolutely right, young lady," he replied. "It seems that I have quite a few gentlemen tasks to take care of."

Maggie giggled. "You're funny."

"Aye, he is at that," Ian agreed with a grin. "You wonder what Mary sees in him."

"He's the police chief," Andy said, coming to the defense of his hero. "He gets the bad guys and he protects us."

Katie wrapped her arm around Andy's shoulders and pulled him to her, placing a kiss on the top of his head. "Yes, he does," she agreed. "And while your father and I are out of town, I want you to listen to Chief Alden, as well as Mary and Ian. Do you understand?"

Squirming slightly, Andy nodded. "Yeah, Mom, I understand," he said. "Sides, if I was bad he could throw me in jail."

Chuckling, Bradley winked at him. "I don't think it will come to that," he said. "Besides, Andy and I are a team, right?"

Andy grinned. "Right. I'm part of Chief Alden's team. See, Mom?"

Hugging both of her children tightly, she nodded. "You both be good, okay?" she said, her voice cracking slightly.

"We will," they promised together.

She kissed them, stood up and faced Mary. "Thank you," she said, her eyes glistening with tears. "I can't tell you..."

Mary stepped up and gave her a hug. "Don't thank me again," she said. "I am really going to enjoy having them stay with me. Now, go home, pack and don't worry about anything."

Katie stepped back, wiped her eyes and nodded.

"So, who wants to see where you're going to sleep?" Ian asked, grabbing their suitcases.

"We do!" Maggie and Andy called, picking up their backpacks and starting toward the staircase.

"Don't forget to say goodbye to your mother," he reminded.

"Bye, Mom," they called over their shoulders as they hurried up the stairs.

With a watery chuckle, she turned to Mary. "Well, I certainly hate these long emotional goodbyes."

Mary laughed. "It just shows they're secure and happy," she said. "Call me anytime you'd like."

Katie nodded. "I will. Thank you."

Once she left, Mary closed the door and turned to Bradley. "She's a very nice lady."

He nodded. "Yeah, and a great mom," he agreed, and then paused for a moment. "I can't believe we've never gone on a date."

"I guess we've been too busy," she said, watching him pull out his cell phone. "What are you...?"

Her cell phone began to ring and she hurried across the room to answer it. "Mary O'Reilly," she said.

"Hi Mary, it's Bradley, Bradley Alden."

She looked across the room, her phone held to her ear and grinned at him. "Oh, Bradley, I think I remember you. A tall fellow, right? Chief of Police?"

He lifted one eyebrow at her. "Thanks for remembering," he said wryly. "I was just wondering if you would be willing to go out with me."

"Like a stake out or something?" she asked.

"No, this would have nothing to do with crime fighting, ghosts or murderers," he explained. "Just a fancy dinner somewhere quiet and romantic."

"Quiet and romantic," she repeated. "That's sounds nice. I have this little black dress I've been dying to wear."

"Um, could we have a date and not use the word 'dying'?" he asked, and met her eyes across the room. "But the thought of you in a little black dress is quite…intriguing."

She giggled. "Let me check my calendar."

She put the phone down on the table, picked up a magazine, flipped through the pages for a moment and then tossed him a sassy look. Picking her phone back up, she grinned at him. "I'm afraid my schedule is pretty booked," she teased. "What date were you considering?"

"Next Saturday?" he asked, leaning against the wall and watching her with amusement.

She walked over to the calendar on her kitchen wall. "Next Saturday, February 13th?" she asked. "The day before Valentine's Day?"

He shrugged. "I figured a girl as pretty as you would already be busy on Valentine's Day."

"Oh, good answer," she replied. "Yes, I think I'll be free on Saturday."

"Excellent," he said, a slow smile spreading over his lips. "I'll pick you up at six-thirty."

She smiled back at him. "I'll be waiting."

He hung up his phone, picked up his coat and walked over to the door. "I'll call you in the morning."

She leaned against the wall in the kitchen and nodded. "That would be nice."

They both heard a crash from upstairs. Mary jumped and Bradley grinned.

"Good luck," he said, slipping out the door.

"Coward," she called after him as she dashed toward the stairs and she was sure she heard him laughing on the other side of the door.

# Chapter Ten

Lights were slipping past her and she felt like she was flying through the air. *This is crazy, if I were flying, I'd be looking down, not up,* she reasoned. *Even Superman flies looking down.*

"Doctor Rachael Lewis, ICU Stat," a tinny voice cracked over the loud speaker.

*Crap, I'm in a hospital,* Mary thought, *I hate hospitals.*

She glanced to her side and saw doorways rushing past her, instead of overhead fluorescent lights. *I'm on a gurney,* she realized, *going down a hallway at top speed. This is not a good thing.*

Suddenly she was in pain. Sharp cramps had her tensing in agony. Her breath was coming out in gasps and her whole body hurt.

"Help me, please," she gasped.

"She's in transition," she heard someone say.

*Transition,* she thought, shaking her head. *No, you're wrong, I can't have a baby, I haven't had sex yet.*

Another pain hit. She screamed. Oh, it hurt so much. Sweat poured from her face. Her whole body shuddered as she tried to control the pain. Then once again, the pain faded for the time being.

"I can't...I can't have a baby," Mary cried, trying to make them understand.

"Don't worry, honey," a comforting voice said. "We're gonna help you deliver that baby."

They wheeled her into a surgery room and lifted her up onto a bed. "Tell me, honey, how long have you been having these pains?" the nice voice said.

"I don't know," she said. "I didn't know I was…"

A fresh wave a contractions hit again. Mary bit her lip hard enough for it to bleed in order to prevent herself from yelling.

"Oh, honey, if you want to scream, you just go ahead and scream," the nice voice said.

"My baby," she whimpered.

"Oh, I think your baby is gonna be fine," she said. "She just got a little stuck, that's all."

Mary felt more pressure and took a deep breath.

"That's it honey, take a couple more of those deep breaths."

Suddenly she needed to push down. "Oh, there you go girl," the voice said. "You know what to do."

"Okay, now, that contraction's over, so you take it easy for a few minutes."

"Where's Bradley?" Mary asked, looking around the stark white delivery room. "I need to see Bradley."

Suddenly Bradley was next to her. "Mary, what are you doing?"

"I'm having a baby," she said. "Our baby."

"But Mary, you can't have a baby," he said. "You can never have a baby."

"No, owwwwwww," she moaned as the next contraction hit.

She reached out for his hand, but it was too far away. "Bradley," she cried. "Help me."

"Honey, you need to concentrate on this baby," the nice voice said. "It wants to be born right away."

"Bradley," she cried.

"Okay honey, bear down and push that baby out."

Mary pushed down with all her might, felt the whoosh of the baby slip from her body. She heard the sound of her baby's cry and tried to lift her arms to hold her.

"My baby," she gasped, looking around to see her child.

A nurse held the swaddled child a few feet away. "I'm sorry Officer O'Reilly, you can't have any children," the nurse said.

"But my baby," Mary cried, trying to push herself off the table to reach her child.

"I'm sorry, Mary," Bradley said, walking away with the nurse. "This is my baby, not yours."

"Bradley," she screamed, tears running down her face. "I want my baby. Give me my baby."

"Sorry, Mary," he said, fading into the bright light of the room. "Just a bad dream…"

"Mary, darling, you have to wake up," Ian urged. "Come on, Mary. It's just a bad dream."

Mary opened her eyes. "Ian, the baby," she said sitting up in her bed, her eyes searching widely around the room. "I can't find the baby."

"I know, darling," he said, placing his hands on her shoulders. "We need to find the baby."

She took a deep shuddering breath. "Will you help me?" she asked with a soft cry.

"Of course I will," he soothed. "I need you to take a deep breath and close your eyes for just a moment first."

"Then we'll find the baby?"

"Yes, darling, I promise," he said.

She closed her eyes and took a deep breath.

"Can you hear me, darling?" he asked.

She nodded.

"Mary, take another deep breath," he said in a soft calming voice. "And think about all the things you love in your bedroom; your big fluffy comforter and your thick comfy pillows. And what color would they be?"

She smiled and took another deep breath. "White," she said. "They're white."

"Aye, I can see that now," he said. "And your home, think about all the things you love in your home. The fireplace, the cozy kitchen…"

He watched her shoulders relax and her breathing deepen.

"The sexy Scot in the next room," he whispered and smiled when he saw her lips turn up. "Where are you, Mary?"

She laid back down and snuggled into her pillow. "I'm in my room, trying to sleep," she murmured. "I'm so tired."

"Aye, sorry I am that I woke you," he said. "I'll just go back to my room and leave you be."

"Mmmmmm-hmmmmm," she mumbled, her breathing deep and rhythmic.

"Good trick, professor," Mike said, looking down at Mary from the end of the bed.

"Did she wake the children?" Ian asked.

Shaking his head, Mike said, "No, you were in here calming her before they had a chance to hear her. Not sleeping too well are you?"

Ian sighed deeply and slipped off the edge of the bed. He stood next to Mike and looked down at Mary. "It's my fault," he said simply. "If I hadn't suggested hypnotism…"

"Jeannine's murderer wouldn't have been found and the creep could have killed another woman," Mike said. "And I'm sure you forced Mary to do this and she didn't twist your arm one little bit."

"Well, I could have said no," he argued.

"You're a smart guy," Mike said. "You understand people pretty well, right?"

Ian nodded.

"Mary's a third generation cop," he said. "She stepped in front of a bullet to save her brother. She doesn't let people tell her what to do. She knew there was risk, but she felt the risk was worth it. Probably still does."

"I hate to see her hurting like this," Ian whispered.

"Yeah, me too," he said. "We just need to make sure we're here when she needs us."

"Aye, I'm not going anywhere."

Mike grinned. "Yeah, I didn't think so. Go to bed, professor, I'll watch over her."

Ian nodded. "Aren't you tired...?"

Mike lifted one eyebrow and Ian shook his head. "Must be more tired than I thought," he said. "Good night, Mike."

"Night, professor."

# Chapter Eleven

Mary was surprised to find Ian already working in the kitchen when she came down the stairs the next morning. Ian looked up from the kitchen table and smiled. "We have a wee bit of time before the bairns need to be up," he said, getting out of his chair. "Would you join me in a cup of tea?"

She nodded. "That would be nice," she said, running her hand through her hair. "I don't feel very rested."

He poured her a cup from the teapot on the counter and carried it to her. "Well, you had a bit of a nightmare last night," he said.

Pausing in the midst of getting a sip of tea, she looked up at him. "A nightmare?" she asked. "Did I wake Andy and Maggie?"

He shook his head and smiled. "No, I only knew because I was listening for you," he said. "I thought your first night home might be a hard one."

She sat at the table and placed her cup down. "I do remember that you were in my room," she said slowly. "I thought it was a dream."

He sat down next to her and grinned. "So, do you oft have dreams about me being in your bedroom?" he asked, wagging his eyebrows.

She chuckled. "No," she said baldly, grinning at his dejected face. "Which is why it stood out as strange."

"Ach, she cuts out me heart and then does a quick Highland fling upon it."

Mary placed her hand on Ian's. "I'm so sorry," she said. "But you are already promised to both Gillian and Maggie. I don't think I can stand the competition."

He placed his hand on top of hers and took a deep breath. "And now, darling, we need to have a serious conversation," he said, his face and the tone of his voice becoming serious.

She nodded.

"I need to understand why you won't let me hypnotize you again," he said. "Can you not trust me anymore?"

Her eyes widened and she shook her head. "Oh, Ian, no," she insisted. "It's nothing like that at all."

He sat back and studied her for a moment. "And if it's not that," he said, "then what's the reason?"

She slipped her hands out from under his, picked up the hot mug of tea and took her time sipping it in order to gather her thoughts. Slowly placing the cup on the table, she lifted her eyes to him. "If you were to hypnotize me, would you be able to pick and choose which memories I'd be able to keep and which ones I'd lose?"

He shook his head. "I couldn't promise that," he said. "The mind is a wily place. There's no telling how things are connected to one another, but I'd have to believe that all of those memories would be linked together."

"That's what I thought," she said. "And that's why I can't allow you to remove them."

"Why?" he asked. "Are you still investigating something on the case?"

She sighed and shrugged. "No, it's...it's ridiculous," she said, "and I don't expect you to understand."

"Try me."

Sitting back in her chair, she met his eyes. "When I was shot, the bullet went through my abdomen," she said. "The doctors patched me up as best they could, and it was literally a miracle that I came through the surgery. But..."

She paused and took a quick breath. "But they didn't know if things were damaged inside of me," she explained. "They didn't know, don't know, if I can ever have children."

"Ahhhh," Ian said. "That perhaps explains your nightmare, you were crying out for your baby."

Wiping a few stray tears, she smiled at him. "I remember it a little. I gave birth to a baby, I felt it, but they kept saying I couldn't have a baby. Bradley took the baby and disappeared with it."

"Your greatest fears," Ian asked. "Losing both Bradley and your baby?"

She shrugged. "I guess that's probably true. But through Jeannine and her memories I got to feel a life growing inside me. I got to give birth to a baby. I got to hear the sound of a baby's first cry. Can you understand how important that is to me?"

He shook his head and leaned forward in his chair, clasping his hand together. "No, I have to admit, I can't," he said. "Mary, this was not your baby. It was Jeannine's baby."

"It was also Bradley's baby and I'm not ready to give that up."

"I'll grant you, you experienced a miracle," he said. "But you also suffered horrors no woman should bear. Are you sure the memory of the birth is worth the anguish?"

She nodded. "I'm sure."

Sitting back in his chair, he took a quick sip of tea. "Well, then," he said. "It looks like we're on to plan B. We need to find ourselves a ghost."

"You're looking for a ghost?" Andy said from the staircase. "Can I help?"

Ian smiled at Mary. "Ah, so we have a ghostbuster in training."

"I'd be real good at finding ghosts," Andy said. "Cause I ain't afraid of nothing. I'm the bravest person I know. 'Cept for Chief Alden."

Ian stood, walked over to the stove and scooped a bowlful of oatmeal out of a pot. "Are you brave enough to eat good Scottish porridge?" he asked.

"Sure," Andy replied. "Long as you let me put good stuff on it."

Ian shuddered. "Americans. Aye, I'll let you have your brown sugar and raisins."

"Can I have some too please?" Maggie asked, making her way into the kitchen dragging her backpack.

"Darling, you may have anything you'd like," Ian said.

Maggie turned to Mary. "I love the way he talks."

Ian placed a bowl of oatmeal in front of both of them. "And I love the way you talk too, darling," he said gently. "Now, eat up and I'll fix your lunches."

Maggie scooped a spoonful into her mouth. "He's a good cooker," she said after a moment.

"It's 'cause he lives in a castle," Andy said. "Castle people know how to make good oatmeal."

"It's porridge," Ian corrected.

Maggie giggled. "That's what the three bears ate," she said.

"Aye, and what Goldilocks ate," Ian said, raising his voice an octave. "This porridge is too hot. This porridge is too cold."

"And this porridge is just right," Maggie added, scooping another spoonful into her mouth.

"Exactly," Ian said, winking at her. "And how do you feel about peanut butter and jelly sandwiches?"

"We love them," Andy said. "'Specially with extra peanut butter."

Maggie nodded, her mouth full of food. "And jelly," she murmured.

"Well, then, extra peanut butter and jelly it is," he said.

Mary got up and went to the pantry. "I have some cookies, potato chips and fruit snacks," she said. "Which would be the best...?"

"Cookies," Andy called. "And chips."

"And fruit snacks," Maggie added.

Mary turned to Ian. "Do we have enough room in the sacks for all three?"

"Oh, aye, there's always room for snacks," he said. "So, Andy, tell me a ghost story."

Andy took another spoonful of oatmeal and swallowed quickly. "There's the ghost who lives at the old library," he said.

Ian turned to Mary and she shook her head. "He was just visiting," she said.

"Well, there's the ghost that lives at the Historical Museum," Andy said.

Mary smiled. "Oh, that's a good one, Andy," she said. "But he only visits occasionally. No unfinished business there."

Andy sighed.

"I know, the ghost at the high school," Maggie said.

"Yeah, the ghost at the high school," Andy repeated. "Good one, Maggie."

Mary was instantly alert. "Tell me about the ghost at the high school," Mary said, grabbing the snacks from the pantry and walking over to the counter and dropping them in the sacks. "Where is it?"

"On the second floor," Andy said, "in the chemistry lab."

Maggie nodded. "Uh huh," she said. "He opens the windows and unlocks the doors."

Mary smiled. "Why would he do that?" she asked.

"'Cause he got stuck in there in a fire," Maggie said, "and got burned up."

"Oh, well, the poor fellow," Ian said.

"Yeah, but he saved all the students," Andy added. "He was a hero. So how come he's a ghost?"

Ian placed the bagged sandwiches into the sacks, folded down the tops and carried them to the table. "Well, that's a very good question, Andy," he said. "And perhaps that's something Mary and I can discover."

Mary looked over at the clock. "You have ten minutes until the bus is here," she said. "Go upstairs and brush your teeth. Then we'll get you bundled up in your coats."

They rushed up the stairs, giggling the entire way. Mary picked up their bowls and brought them over to the sink. "Well, what do you think?" she asked.

"I think we did well for a couple of amateurs," Ian said, picking up the sacks and putting them in their backpacks.

Mary laughed. "No, I meant about the ghost. It sounds like Dr. Thorne's father," she said. "Although I have to say, you did a wonderful job this morning."

He grinned. "You get to cook tomorrow morning."

"I'll just have to bribe Rosie to bring over cinnamon rolls," she said, rinsing out the pan.

"You'll get no argument from me," Ian said. "She cooks like an angel."

Mary laughed. "I do recall you proposing to her so she'd cook for you," she said, filling the sink with soap and hot water. "I'd hate to have both Stanley and Maggie upset. Do you think you can control yourself?"

"Aye, I'll control myself," he said. "She's a promised woman now."

"I wonder if Rosie or Stanley have heard about this ghost," Mary said.

The clatter of feet on the staircase and young voices raised in argument interrupted their conversation. "Can too," Maggie said.

"Can not!" Andy argued.

Maggie ran over to Ian, her eyes filled with tears. "Andy said I can't marry you 'cause you live in a castle and since I'm not a princess I can't live in a castle too."

Ian knelt down in front of her, brushed her hair away from her face and helped her into her coat. "Well, darling, from what I can see you look like a princess to me," he said. "So I suppose that settles it."

She beamed at him and then turned to her brother. "See, Ian says I'm a princess."

Andy rolled his eyes. "Yeah, but…"

Mary knelt down in front of Andy, zipping up the front of his coat. "And if Maggie is a princess, it must mean that you are either a prince or a knight of the realm," she said. "So, you could visit Ian's castle too."

"For real?" Andy asked, pulling his cap over his ears.

"Aye," Ian said. "I'm sure I have a sword sitting around the place that'd suit you just fine."

"Cool!" Andy said, beaming at his sister. "You can get married to him and I'll be the guard."

Maggie smiled, pulling her mittens on as Ian placed her hat on her head. "Kay."

The honk of the bus's horn interrupted the conversation. "Come on, Maggie, let's go."

"Bye!" they yelled as they ran out the front door.

"Bye," Mary and Ian called, collapsing into the kitchen chairs after the door closed.

"So, are we going to be able to do a week of this?" Mary asked.

Ian grinned. "Do we have a choice?"

# Chapter Twelve

Bradley sat down at his desk and looked at the mess surrounding him. During the time he'd spent out of the office watching over Mary, the paperwork seemed to have multiplied threefold. He started to sort the piles into priorities when the phone rang.

"Chief Alden," he said into the receiver.

"Hey, it's Sean."

Bradley sat back in his chair. "Hey, I'm sorry. I forgot to call you yesterday," he said. "Mary's out of the hospital. She came home yesterday."

"Yeah, she called me last night," he said. "How's she doing, really?"

Bradley took a deep breath. "Well, physically she's worn out, but other than that, she's good. But she's having some flashbacks."

"What kind of flashbacks?"

Bradley ran his hand through his hair. "Rape flashbacks."

"What the hell?" Sean yelled. "She was raped? I should have let you kill the bastard. Never mind, I'll kill him myself."

"Wait, Sean, it's not exactly what you think."

"How the hell can it not be what I think? She's having rape flashbacks."

"Did you know about the hypnosis Ian performed on her?"

"What?"

"The only way they could help Jeannine recover her memory was to hypnotize her, but the only way they could do that was have Mary allow Jeannine to use her body to get hypnotized," he explained. "So Mary lived through everything Jeannine experienced."

There was silence on the other end for a few moments. "When will she stop throwing herself in front of every bullet she sees?" he said quietly.

Bradley sighed. "I'm hoping it's when she becomes my wife."

"What the...?" Sean sputtered. "You actually asked her?"

"Well, yeah I did," Bradley admitted. "But she was still asleep."

Sean burst out laughing. "Oh, yeah, that's the way to do it. Propose when she's unconscious."

"It just slipped out," he admitted. "It seemed like the thing to do at the time."

"So, did you ask her again? Now that she's awake?"

Bradley leaned forward and rested his head in his hand. "No, I haven't. I want to give her some time to recover and..."

"What?"

"I want to ask your father permission for her hand in marriage."

"Hey, that's nice."

"It's what gentlemen do," he said, his lips turned up in a smile.

"Yeah, well, you tell me when and I'll make sure all the O'Reilly men are present," Sean said.

"Thanks," Bradley replied wryly. "Thanks a lot!"

"No problem," he teased.

There was another pause, but this time when Sean spoke there was no laughter in his voice.

"Bradley, actually I called because I got the judge's order. We can exhume the body, I mean Jeannine, tomorrow."

Bradley's breath caught in his throat and his stomach clenched. "Tomorrow?"

"Yeah, well, we can put it off if you want."

He shook his head. "No, no, she's waited long enough and I can't search for the baby until we get her identity clarified," he said. "I have just been so busy with Mary; I haven't spoken with Jeannine's parents yet."

"Like I said, we could wait."

"Listen, let's go ahead and schedule it for tomorrow, afternoon, okay?" he said. "I'll drive down to her parents today and talk to them. If I need to reschedule, I'll let you know."

"Yeah, that sounds good," he replied. "Bradley, I'm sorry. I know this is going to be rough."

"Yeah, but I'm hoping they'll at least feel some closure, knowing where she is."

"Good luck."

"Thanks, Sean."

# Chapter Thirteen

Mary sat at her desk in her living room flipping through her old address book. There was a fire crackling in the fireplace and Ian was sitting on the couch working on his laptop. She located a number and typed the name into her computer and hit the "Enter" button to perform a search. "Yes!" she said, throwing her fist up in the air.

Ian looked up at Mary over his reading glasses and smiled. "You found a contact?"

She nodded. "Yes, a fellow from DCFS I dated a couple of times."

"Is he still talking to you after you broke it off with him?"

She shifted on her chair and turned to him. "How would you know that I broke it off with him?" she asked. "He might have dumped me."

Grinning, he shook his head. "Only if he were a fool, both blind and daft."

"You say the nicest things," she replied, her cheeks turning slightly red.

"Ach, Mary, me love, I only speak the truth," he replied, his eyes twinkling. "And would you be thinking about making lunch this afternoon?"

She snorted. "Okay, you just ruined everything," she said. "All that sweet talking for a bowl of chili."

"Is it chili you'd be making for lunch today?" he said, shifting on the couch. "Well, that's a meal a man can get used to having daily. Would you be making those wee corn muffins with it?"

She laughed. "Yes, I can make corn muffins too," she said. "Let me make this call first, then I'll get things going for lunch."

He looked back down at his computer screen and started tapping on the keyboard. "Just so you know," he said, not looking at her. "The food had nothing to do with the statement about the laddie. You're a fair bonnie lass, Mary O'Reilly."

"Thank you, Ian MacDougal," she replied. "And you're a fine braw laddie yourself."

He raised his eyes over his glasses and stared at her, surprised.

"What? Do you think you're the only one who can speak Scottish?" she asked.

Grinning, he lowered his eyes to the screen. "The Internet is a grand place, isn't it Mary?"

She chuckled. "Aye, it is, Ian."

"Speaking of the Internet," Ian said. "I've done a bit of research into the explosion at the high school. Sean's been helpful getting some fire records opened for me."

"And?" Mary asked.

"It's a strange bit of work, here," he said. "The initial fire report has been redacted, all kinds of interesting black marks appearing on the pages, especially when the fire investigator is looking for a secondary incendiary device."

"Really," she said. "And what is the conclusion?"

"Ach, well, there is no conclusion," he said. "Because the case involved chemicals that were purchased from a local manufacturing company, they brought their own team in to investigate the fire. They ruled it an accident and stated the only secondary explosion was the cause of the teacher's experiment in the front of the room."

"And you're suspicious?"

Ian chuckled. "Darling, I'm a researcher, I'm always suspicious. It'd be grand to learn more about what happened that night."

"I'm up for a field trip," Mary said. "We could get Rosie and Stanley to babysit for a bit."

"Sounds like a cunning plan," Ian agreed. "You make your calls and then let's invite Rosie and Stanley over."

She picked up her phone and dialed the Chicago number. In a moment the phone was answered.

"Harold Weller."

"Hello Hal. This is Mary O'Reilly," she replied. "Do you remember me?"

"Oh… wow… um… Mary… wow… Mary O'Reilly," the voice on the phone nervously replied. "Yes…of course, of course I do. How are you, Mary?"

"I'm great, Hal, just great. How are you?" Mary asked, picking up a pencil and tapping it on her notepad.

"I'm… Wow… Mary, it's so good to hear from you. Are you in town? Maybe we could get together…"

Mary smiled and glanced over at Ian who seemed caught up in his work. *Good*, she thought.

"That would be great, Harold. It's really been a long time, but unfortunately, I'm not in Chicago. I'm still in Freeport."

"Oh, yeah, what in the world made you move that far away? I, I mean, we all miss you."

"Well, you know, after the shooting and all, I decided I needed some time away from the big city," she explained.

"Oh, that's right. I'm so sorry. I totally forgot about that," he stammered. "Are you okay?"

*Yes, but I'll never be able to play the piano again*, she thought wickedly to herself. *Of course, I never could play it in the first place.*

"Well, you know, there were some residual effects," she said. "But for the most part, I'm good. I opened up a small private investigation agency."

"Wow, that's great," he replied. "How's it going?"

"Well, that's one of the reasons for my call," she said. "Besides touching base with you after all this time."

"Yeah, it's so great to talk to you again," he replied. "What can I do to help you?"

Mary turned the pencil in her hand and poised it for writing. "Well, this is such a long shot," she explained. "And really, I don't even know if you can help me. But when I encountered this issue, the first person I thought of was you. You always seemed to know your way around things there at DCFS."

"Well, you know, I do my best."

"Well, that's what I'm going to need," she said. "My client just found out his wife was kidnapped and murdered. While under the control of the kidnapper, she gave birth to a daughter at Cook County Hospital. The kidnapper posed as her husband and gave the child up to DCFS for adoption. He's trying to find his daughter."

"Oh, wow, that's crazy," Harold replied. "Can you give me some dates?"

Mary gave him the information and heard him entering it into his computer.

"Does your client have any evidence yet?" he asked.

"Well, the kidnapper confessed, but he's still awaiting a court date," she replied. "And they are exhuming his wife's body in the next few days. So, he's waiting for all of the legal work to get done. Oh, he's also a cop."

"Wow, okay, yeah, let me see what I can do."

She waited a few more minutes.

"Mary, these papers, they're sealed up tight," he said. "I don't have a lot of information. Only the date of the adoption and the case worker assigned to follow up. But, okay, here's what I can tell you."

He paused again.

"Freeport," he said.

"Yes, I live in Freeport," Mary replied, "but what about the little girl?"

"Okay, well, that's crazy," he said. "The case worker that was assigned for follow-up, Kat Tinder, she was in the Freeport Office. So, the little girl must have gone to the Freeport area."

Mary dropped her pencil on the desk and sat up straight. "You're kidding me?" she exclaimed. "She's in Freeport?"

Ian sat up and stared at Mary.

"Do you have anything else?"

"No, sorry, Mary," he replied. "But let me get a requisition and try to pull the original file. It's going to take a while because it comes from the archives in Springfield, but I'll get it to you as soon as I can."

"Hal, you are wonderful," she said, after giving him her contact information. "Thanks so much."

"Hey, you ever get back in town?" he asked. "We could do lunch."

Smiling, she nodded. "Yeah, that would be nice. I'll call you next time I'm there."

"Thanks Mary," he said. "Good luck with your client."

"Yeah, well, at least we know where she lives."

"Where she lived eight years ago," he reminded her.

"Oh, yeah, that's true. Thanks again, Hal. Bye."

She hung up the phone in a slight daze and turned to Ian. "Bradley's little girl was adopted by a family who lived in Freeport," she said, shaking her head. "How weird is that?"

Putting his laptop down on the coffee table, Ian shook his head. "Actually, I don't find it weird at all."

She turned her chair to face him and folded her arms over her chest. "Excuse me, Mr. Professor; you don't think that's strange?"

He grinned. "Okay Mary, you and I already deal in a, let's call it, psychic world. We understand there's more to our existence than most people do, right?"

She nodded.

"And we've heard those stories about families moving and their pets getting lost, but eight months later the pet shows up on the doorstep, hundreds of miles away."

"Yeah, but what does that…?"

"There are psychic connections that we haven't even begun to explore," he interrupted. "The mother who knows her son has been shot in a war thousands of miles away. The infant who stops crying once he feels his mother's touch. The husband who begins to pick up the phone seconds before it rings because he knows his wife is calling."

"Okay, but what does that…?"

Ian lifted his hand to stop her. "A father who desperately searches for his wife and daughter is led to the town where his daughter lives," he said, and then continued pointedly looking at her. "A woman searching for new meaning in her life is led to a town where she can reunite a father and daughter. Psychic connections."

"I prefer to think some of these things are guided by God," she replied.

Ian shrugged his shoulders. "I'm not saying they're not. Why wouldn't God use these gifts in order to help people communicate on a higher plane?"

Mary ran her hand through her hair one more time. "This is a lot to consider," she said, standing up. "I think I need chocolate."

Ian stood and followed her to the kitchen. "Aye, good idea. But then, we need chili."

# *Chapter Fourteen*

Bradley drove the cruiser down Galena Avenue, stopping at the light on South Street and then turning left toward Highway 20. The day was cold and overcast and everything seemed to be wearing a shroud of grey. It seemed even Mother Nature was acknowledging Jeannine's death.

Her parents had been a little confused with his request to meet with them. He didn't want to tell them anything until he was there in person, instead needing to look into their eyes and explain what he'd learned about her death. He owed them that much at least.

He drove past Springfield Street and merged onto Highway 20. The road, as usual, was fairly empty during the midday hours. He leaned forward to press the cruise control button when a slight movement out of the corner of his eye, caught his attention. He turned quickly to find Mike sitting in the passenger's seat.

"Holy shit," he yelled, swerving the car into the left lane.

"Really? You're a law enforcement professional and you drive like this?" Mike asked. "I'm surprised you even have a license."

"What the hell do you think you're doing?" Bradley asked.

Mike shrugged. "Going with you. I figured you could use the company."

Shaking his head, Bradley was momentarily confused. "You're going with me?"

"Yeah, a guy shouldn't have to be alone at a time like this," he said.

Bradley gripped the steering wheel, stared straight ahead and didn't speak for a few minutes. "Thank you, Mike," he finally said, his voice cracking. "I appreciate it."

"Hey, no problem," he said. "So, have you thought about what you're going to say?"

Sighing, Bradley shrugged. "I've practiced this over in my head about a hundred times. But no matter how I say it, I know they are going to be devastated."

Mike nodded. "Yeah, even when you're kind of expecting it, hearing the words out loud can be overwhelming."

Bradley nodded. "Yeah, it can," he said. "I can still remember the shock I felt when I saw Jeannine at Mary's place."

"You were pretty much an idiot about it," Mike said.

"Yeah, I was."

"But you're a guy. We're supposed to be idiots on occasion. It helps women feel superior."

Bradley snorted. "Oh, that's why we do it."

"Keeps the world turning, bro, keeps the world turning."

"So, can I ask, how did your parents take the news about your death?"

Mike turned and looked out the window for a moment, and then he turned back to Bradley. "I don't know," he said. "I wasn't there for them. I didn't know I was dead, so I was at Yellow Creek fishing. I could have fished for an eternity."

Bradley glanced over at him. "I don't understand. How could you just fish and not realize something was wrong?"

"It's a time thing," Mike explained. "When you're dead, you can't comprehend the passage of time, like you do when you're alive. A year to you could be like ten minutes to a ghost. So, we don't have the same urgency as you."

"So, Jeannine…"

"Yeah, she waited a while for you to find her," Mike said. "But it was more like you being late for dinner rather than waiting for years."

"Well that makes me feel a little better," he acknowledged.

"But you still feel like you let her down, right?"

Bradley nodded. "Yeah, how can I feel any other way? And now I get to go tell her parents I let her down."

Mike turned in his seat and faced Bradley. "You know, I'm not saying you shouldn't grieve for her, because you have to do that. But you've got to stop thinking you're as powerful as God."

"What? I don't think…"

"Sure you do," Mike interrupted. "You think you should have prevented what happened to her. You should have known your crazy neighbor would decide to kidnap her. You should have been at the hospital when the doctor injected the drug that accidentally killed her."

"No, that's not what I think."

"Oh, really? Then how can you say you failed her?"

Bradley didn't say anything for a while. He changed lanes and passed a milk truck, and then moved back into the right lane. "I'm alive and she's dead," he whispered. "How am I supposed to feel?"

"Like crap. Like the world isn't fair. Like you got the raw end of the deal," Mike said. "Even mad as hell. But taking her death on yourself is not going to help anyone, least of all you. I should know."

"What do you mean by that?"

"When I was ten years old I lived out in the country. My family had a dairy farm. My dad and my uncles had run it together ever since my grandpa had been killed when a tractor flipped on him. Because Dad was the only one with kids, we got to live in the old farmhouse. It was a great place to grow up."

Taking a deep breath, Mike paused for a moment.

"I had this friend, Timmy Beck," he said. "We were inseparable. We went fishing, played baseball, slept out overnight in my tree house. I knew we were going to be friends forever. So then one summer day Timmy and I were supposed to go fishing together. It was a safer world back then, but we always had the buddy system, you know, we always go as a team. So Timmy gets to my house, he's carrying his fishing pole and tackle box. I start to pick up my stuff when my mom calls me. I was supposed to clean the chicken coop and she just discovered I didn't do it."

"It's amazing how moms find those things out," Bradley said.

Mike smiled slightly. "Yeah, she had ESP where I was concerned. So, I got in trouble and had to go clean out the coop instead of going fishing with Timmy."

"Sounds reasonable."

"Yeah, but instead of going back home, Timmy decides to go fishing by himself."

Turning away from Bradley, Mike looked out the window for a few moments. "They found his body a couple of days later," he said softly. "He'd been molested and then strangled to death. My best friend. If only I'd cleaned the chicken coop when I was supposed to, he wouldn't have died."

"You don't know that," Bradley said. "You both could have been victims."

"Yeah, it took me a long time to figure out that I didn't kill my best friend and I wasn't responsible," he said. "But I was messed up for a long time."

"So, did they find the bastard?"

Mike nodded. "Yeah, turns out the school bus driver did it. I couldn't believe it, he was such a nice guy. But they found a bunch of stuff from all of the victims. Four boys were killed that summer."

"You don't expect something like that to happen in a small town."

"Yeah, almost makes it worse when it's one of your neighbors, one of your friends."

Bradley took a deep breath. "Yes. Yes it is."

# Chapter Fifteen

"So you have those two adorable Brennan children staying with you?" Rosie asked, as Stanley helped her slip out of her coat.

Nodding, Mary closed the door behind them. "Yes, for at least a couple of days. Katie called me this morning, the surgery went well, but recovery isn't going as well as they'd hoped. So I might be able to keep for a little longer."

"Keep 'em," Stanley growled. "It ain't like they's puppies or kittens."

"No, they are much more fun to play with," Mary laughed. "They are so incredibly clever and little Maggie has the biggest crush on Ian. It's so cute."

"Ah, well, the feelings mutual, I assure you," Ian said, coming into the room and sitting on the couch's arm.

"No matter what age, them dames will fall for a foreigner more times than not," Stanley said, walking over to Ian.

"So, it's not my sparkling personality?" Ian asked in mock dismay. "She just loves my accent?"

"Harrumph," Stanley muttered. "If you can't speak English you shouldn't be living here in America."

"Um, begging your pardon, Stanley," Ian inserted. "But I do believe that we invented English before America was even considered a country."

"Yep, and we beat the pants offen you and your countrymen during the Revolutionary War."

"Actually, many Scots fought with America against the British."

Stanley paused. "You don't say."

Ian nodded. "Aye, we've a long friendship with your country."

"Well, then, I take it back," Stanley said. "Now, iffen you could only learn to talk without that accent, things would be fine."

"Ach, well, I'll see what I can do about it," Ian said with a grin. "Would you all be wanting a bit of tea?"

"Oh, yes, Ian, that would be lovely," Rosie said. "And then you must tell me what I can do to help with those dear children."

Mary grinned at Ian. "I thought they might like some cinnamon rolls," she said. "If you have the time to make them."

"Well, yes, of course I do," Rosie said. "I can make some this evening and bring them over. All you'll have to do is reheat them for breakfast."

Shaking his head, Ian turned on the kettle and then walked back over to Rosie. He lifted her hand and placed a kiss on it. "Rosie, please, leave Stanley and run away with me," he pleaded.

Rosie blushed and giggled. "Oh, Ian, you silly boy."

"Rosie, you and your cooking have captured my heart," he said.

Stanley came over and put his arm around Rosie, guiding her to a seat on the couch and sitting next to her. "You can just find your own sweetheart," he grumbled. "This one's taken."

Rosie wrapped her hand around Stanley's arm and smiled up at him. "And she's very happy about being taken too."

Mary sat down on the recliner and smiled at her two friends. It was so nice to see them both so obviously in love.

"So, how are you feeling?" Rosie asked Mary.

"I'm good," she replied. "I've promised to take things easy for a while. Ian and I are going to find a ghost who isn't connected to a murder to help."

"Aye, that reminds me," Ian said. "Have either of you heard about the ghost at the high school?"

Stanley shrugged. "I heard about the ghost in the theater, is that the one?"

"No, this one is supposed to be in the school, on the second floor," Mary said.

The kettle started to whistle, and Ian got up and took it off the stove.

"He's supposed to be a chemistry teacher," he added from the kitchen.

Rosie looked up, her face white. "A chemistry teacher?" she stammered.

"Rosie, what's wrong?" Stanley asked.

She turned to Stanley, her eyes wide. "I didn't know," she said. "I thought he would rest in peace. He's been a ghost…"

"Who, Rosie? Who's been a ghost?" Mary asked.

Turning back to Mary, Rosie clasped her hands together. "Mr. Thorne. He was my chemistry teacher when I was a senior at the high school. I was there when he died."

# Chapter Sixteen

The house looked the same as it had when he had picked Jeannine up for Senior Prom. The shutters were still painted a cranberry red, the siding was soft brown and the window boxes were dark green. It looked like a house that should have been tucked away in the woods, not in the middle of town. Bradley pulled the car into the driveway and quickly switched off the ignition.

"It's better to just go in there and get it over with," Mike said. "They're waiting for some kind of explanation."

Bradley nodded. "Yeah, you're right," he said.

He climbed out of the car and strode the few yards to the front door. It was opened before he could knock. Mike was right – they had been waiting for him.

"Thanks for seeing me on such short notice," he said to Jeannine's parents.

They ushered him into the house and back to the kitchen. It was the place they had always sat and talked. They sat at the table and no one spoke for a moment, not knowing how to move forward. "Would you like a sandwich or something?" Joyce, Jeannine's mother, finally asked.

He shook his head. "Thanks, Joyce, I'm fine."

"How do you like that job up north?" Bill, Jeannine's father, asked.

"I like it," Bradley responded. "I've met a lot of new people and..."

He paused.

"And it's good to be working again," Bill finished. "Isn't it son?"

Nodding, Bradley felt a lump in his throat. "Yes, it feels good to be working again. So, how are you two doing?"

"We're doing just fine," Joyce said. "Bill had a wonderful garden last summer. He has such a green thumb."

"And Joyce joined a computer class at the junior college," Bill added. "She's quite a geek now."

Joyce chuckled. "We actually have e-mail now, Bradley."

"Yes, we are thinking of turning that third bedroom into a computer room," Bill added.

The third bedroom. Jeannine's bedroom, which had been sitting untouched for eight years. A shrine to their missing child.

An uncomfortable silence fell over the room. Joyce reached over and put her hand on Bradley's hand. He realized that it was wrinkled and fragile looking. *They both look older*, he thought. *How long has it been since I've seen them? Three years?*

"I don't know if we ever expressed to you how grateful we were to you for giving up your life to try and find Jeannine for all those years," she said.

He put his other hand on top of her frail one. "I… It was the only thing I could do," he said.

"We want you to know that we realize you did all you could to find her," Bill said. "No one would have sacrificed as much as you did."

Bradley met Bill's eyes. "Thank you, that means a lot to me."

Another few moments of silence. Then Bradley cleared his throat, but before he could speak Bill took a deep breath and saved Bradley from being the one who brought up the topic.

"And we assume the reason you called us is because you have some news," Bill added.

Once again, he nodded his head. "Last week, through an intense investigation, we were able to discover that Jeannine had been kidnapped by someone who lived in our neighborhood. He held her in a subterranean room under his office in downtown Sycamore. He was delusional and thought our baby was his."

Joyce clapped her hand over her mouth. "Oh, my baby," she cried, hope warring with pain. "Down in the dark for all these years."

Bradley closed his eyes for a moment and then turned to Joyce. "No, he only kept her there until she went into labor."

"But that would have been eight years ago," Bill said. "What happened?"

"When she started labor he drove her to Cook County Hospital where she gave birth to…to our daughter," his voice cracked and he put his head on his hand for a moment.

"So, he brought her to a hospital," Joyce repeated. "Surely they must have seen that something was wrong. Surely she was able to ask for help."

"The kidnapper had access to pharmaceuticals and he kept Jeannine drugged for most of the time she was with him. I understand she tried to communicate with the staff, but she was in the throes of labor and they didn't understand what she was trying to say."

"But if they had her medical records," Bill said.

"The hospital was under the impression she was the wife of the kidnapper, so they did not have the correct medical history," he continued slowly. "Then they were concerned about hemorrhaging after the baby was born, so they gave her a shot of Syntometrine."

"But she's allergic…" Bill's voice died out.

Bradley nodded. "She went into cardiac arrest and died in the labor room. The kidnapper had her buried in a small cemetery in Chicago."

Both parents were openly weeping. Bill placed his arm around his wife and held her against his chest. "She's gone," Joyce cried. "Our baby is dead."

"We had always considered…" Bill wept softly. "We always knew she could be…"

"But we'd always hoped," Joyce sobbed. "We'd always prayed…"

"I'm so sorry," Bradley whispered. "I wish..."

Bill pulled a handkerchief out of his pocket, wiped his eyes and took a shuddering breath. "You did all you could, son," he said. "And we are so grateful to you for finally finding out what happened to Jeannine."

Joyce raised her tear-stained face and nodded. "She always loved you," she stammered. "You were always her one and only true love."

"I loved her with all my heart," he said.

"But..." Joyce stared at Bradley and then turned and looked at her husband. "But she gave birth to a baby. We have a grandchild."

"What happened to the baby?" Bill asked.

"The kidnapper handed her over to DCFS to put up for adoption," he said. "I'm trying to get the court to order a release of those documents, so I can find her."

"What can we do to help?" Bill asked. "Do you need money, a lawyer?"

Shaking his head, Bradley explained, "I've met some really good people in Freeport who have connections to the Chicago Police Force and they have been very instrumental in moving things forward."

"Where is she buried?" Bill asked. "Can we see the grave?"

"She was buried under the kidnapper's wife's name. I received a call this morning that the judge has signed the papers to have her body exhumed, but before we did that, I wanted to talk to you, so we could plan the next steps," he said.

"Do you... Could we be there when they open the grave?" Joyce asked.

Bradley nodded. "Yes, you can. We'll probably need her dental records to identify her, but if you feel it would help you. You should be there."

"It's not the last image I want to remember, but I think we need to go," Bill said. "For Jeannine."

Joyce nodded. "Yes, we need to be there for our baby."

"After they remove her and are able to verify she is Jeannine, we can make sure she is laid to rest properly," he said. "I wondered if there was a place..."

"Yes, yes, we already have a plot for her," Bill said. "We bought it a few years ago, next to our plots in the cemetery. We bought one for you too."

"So we could all be together," Joyce added.

"Thank you," Bradley said. "That was very thoughtful of you and I know she will be happy to be in familiar surroundings."

"I'll get in touch with our funeral director today and see about getting this arranged for a memorial service. Could we... Do you think we could have one next weekend?"

Bradley nodded. "Yes, I'll call Sean and let him know that's what we are planning."

Joyce sniffled and shook her head. "You know, it's funny, in the past few months I've felt Jeannine's presence occasionally here at the house. It was as if she were visiting us. But last week that feeling went away. I suppose she's finally at peace."

Bradley recalled Jeannine's face as she said her final goodbye to him. "Yes," he whispered. "I'm sure she is."

# *Chapter Seventeen*

"I was Rosie Meriwether back then," Rosie said, dabbing a tissue delicately against her eyes. "I remember like it was yesterday. First Coach Thorne gave a demonstration and then we all had lab work to do. Something went wrong and one of the experiments exploded and started a fire. Then, pretty soon, the whole classroom was filled with flames. Coach Thorne and one of the boys, Stevo Morris, ran to the windows and helped us all get out. Coach Thorne had just helped Stevo out when the whole room exploded. It was awful."

"But why didn't you just go out the doors?" Mary asked.

"They were all locked," Rosie said.

Ian shot Mary a questioning glance and then turned to Rosie. "Was that common practice? Locking the classroom doors?"

Shaking her head, Rosie's eyes widened. "You know, I never thought of that before, but no, we never locked the doors."

Ian picked up a notepad and started to write some things down. "How long had he been teaching chemistry?"

"Oh, he'd been at the school for about ten years," Rosie said. "He was probably getting close to tenure."

"That's interesting," Mary said. "I wonder if there were only a few slots open for tenure. It would be interesting to find out who his competition was."

Nodding, Ian made a quick note and looked at Rosie. "You called him Coach Thorne?"

"Yes, he was the baseball coach," she replied. "His team had gone to State five years in a row. No one could beat him."

Ian looked over to Mary. "Okay, that's another possibility."

"Possibility for what?" Stanley asked.

"Until we talk to him, I can't be sure. But I think there was more to this accident than meets the eye."

"Someone did this on purpose," Rosie said with a shiver. "His wife was right."

Ian looked up from his notes. "What?"

"His wife always said he was too careful, he wouldn't have made a mistake with the chemicals," Rosie said. "I remember overhearing her at the funeral luncheon. She wanted the police to look into it. But they only patted her on the shoulder and told her it was an accident."

"I remember reading about it," Stanley said. "They figured something was wrong with the chemicals. The B&R Company looked into it. That Caleb Brandlocker, he stood behind his products. Hired themselves a specialist to look into it, turns out it was just one of those things."

"Who's Brandlocker?" Ian asked. "Are they the chemical company?"

"They are one of the largest manufacturers in the area," Mary explained. "They started out over 100 years ago and their salesmen went door to door in horse-pulled specialty wagons that had a large supply of their products. They sold everything from horse liniment to women's shampoo. They have been one of the biggest manufacturers here for over a hundred years."

"So, they also hire the most people in the area," Ian said. "A bit of political pull?"

"Oh, hell, Caleb didn't need political pull," Stanley said. "He was the head of the school board. All he had to do was pass a resolution. His son, Ephraim, is the head of the board now and the president of the company."

"I think it's time we meet Coach Thorne, Mary," Ian said.

Mary smiled. "I think that's a really good idea," she agreed.

"Hold your horses," Stanley said. "Ain't the reason you was taking this case is because it weren't supposed to be about murder? Seems to me you're looking for trouble again."

Mary shook her head. "Stanley, this happened over forty years ago. Do you really think someone is going to be worried about us looking into it?"

"Well, you just never know what some people are thinking," Stanley said, his eyebrows lifting nearly to the top of his forehead. "And I know of one police chief who wouldn't be too happy if he found out you was messing with a possible murder."

Mary sighed. "Well, we don't even know it's a murder yet," she argued. "Really, we need to talk to Coach Thorne before we all jump to the worst possible conclusion."

"So, how do we get into the high school and talk with him?" Ian asked.

Rosie lifted her hand and waved it. "Oh, I know," she said. "Tonight the Speech Team has practice and they leave the door open for the kids to get in. All you have to do is go in the office door and go up to the second floor. The chemistry labs are around the corner and down the hall from where the team meets."

"What do you think, Stanley?" Mary asked.

"Well, I reckon it don't hurt none to talk to the man, I mean the ghost," he said. "Then we can decide. But we don't, none of us, need to mention what we're doing to anyone else."

"Why, Stanley, of course I don't," she said. "My lips are sealed."

Mary grinned. "Thank you, Rosie," she said. "Now, how do you feel about babysitting for a little while this evening?"

Clapping her hands together, Rosie beamed. "That will be just the thing," she said. "I'll bring over the ingredients and we can make cinnamon rolls together."

Mary turned to Ian. "So, professor, you want to go ghost hunting with me tonight?"

He grinned back at her. "Aye, sounds like a rare good time."

# Chapter Eighteen

Bradley came back into the kitchen, placing his phone in his pocket. "I just got off the phone with the coroner's office," he said to the man sitting at the table next to Jeannine's parents. "They would like at least a week time to make sure they get good results, they can release Jeannine's body to you next Friday morning."

Allen Henderson, the local funeral director, stood and nodded solemnly. "Thank you, I'll have a hearse there first thing in the morning to transport her back to Sycamore. Is there anything else you need?"

"No, thank you," Bradley said. "You've been very helpful."

"I'd like to think about the wording of her obituary a little longer," Joyce said. "Can I send it to you later this afternoon?"

"Of course," Allen said. "And we'll have it run in the paper on Thursday with the announcement of the memorial service."

"Do we need to contact the cemetery?" Bill asked.

"I'll do that," Allen said. "You've already paid for the plot, so we just need to work out the details of having things ready for Saturday."

He gathered his paperwork and then shook hands with each of them. "I'm so sorry it turned out like this," he said. "We all hoped…"

Joyce wiped a stray tear from her cheek. "Yes, we did," she said. "But at least we know what happened and we can finally let her rest."

Allen nodded. "Well, if there is anything else I can do, please don't hesitate to ask."

"Thanks, Allen, we appreciate it," Bradley said. "See you on Saturday."

After Allen left, Bradley walked to the front door with Joyce and Bill. "I need to go back to Freeport and take care of some things, but I'll see you both tomorrow."

"We'll meet you at the coroner's office at noon," Joyce said. "Will that work?"

Bradley nodded. "That would be great. Thank you."

"You know, we will always consider you to be our son," Bill said. "And once you find your daughter, we will be thrilled to spoil her."

Smiling, Bradley hugged them both. "She couldn't ask for a better set of grandparents."

Mike remained silent until Bradley had pulled the cruiser out of the driveway and was headed back toward Freeport. "Those are great people," he said.

"Yeah, they are," Bradley agreed.

"So, how are you holding up?" Mike asked.

Staring straight ahead, he tightened his hold on the steering wheel. "I'm holding on," he said.

"I've just got to get through these next couple of days and I'll be good."

"You're an idiot," Mike replied casually.

"What?"

"Is that where Jeannine is going to be buried?" Mike asked, pointing to a large cemetery down the road.

"Yeah, it is," Bradley said.

"Pull in there."

"Why?"

"Don't ask questions, just do it," Mike said.

Bradley glowered at Mike, but did as he requested. "What, is there a ghost in here we need to help?" he asked, pulling the cruiser to the side of a lane and putting it in park.

"Come on, let's take a walk," Mike said.

"A walk? It's freezing out there."

"Yeah, a walk," he said, slipping through the car door.

A moment later Bradley joined him and they walked across the cemetery until they reached a small stone bench.

"Sit down on the bench and talk to me," Mike said.

"What the hell?"

"This is one of the only places where a grown man can be seen talking to himself and people won't think he's nuts," Mike explained. "So, talk to me."

"About what?"

"About Jeannine. Tell me how you met her. Tell me about your first date. Tell me about the day you found out she was pregnant."

Bradley sat down on the bench and stared at Mike. "Why are you doing this?" he asked, his voice breaking.

"Tell me," Mike insisted.

Bradley took a deep breath. "Okay, I first met Jeannine when we were both in high school," he began. "She was...she was... Oh, God...she's gone. I'm never going to see her again."

He bent over and placed his head in his hands as the sorrow washed over him. Tears he had been holding back for eight years broke free and poured from his eyes. His body was wracked in shudders of emotion and he was helpless to stop it. He pictured her on their first date, on their wedding day and when she announced she was pregnant. All their plans, all of their happiness, everything was gone and she was never coming back.

After a while, the shuddering eased and he took deep gulping breaths of air.

"Feeling better?" Mike asked.

Wiping his eyes and nose with a handkerchief, he looked up at Mike. "Why?"

"Because you've been strong for a long time and you needed to grieve."

"I had to be strong," he whispered. "I didn't want to let my feelings out."

"Yeah, I get that," Mike agreed. "You had to be strong for Jeannine, for her parents and for your daughter. You had to be strong until you found her."

Bradley nodded his head deliberately. "I still can't believe she's gone," he said. "My whole life had been centered on finding her and now…"

"And now you have to figure out who you are without her," he said.

"How the hell do you know this stuff? You were a fireman."

Mike shrugged. "I had a youth minister who talked to me about this stuff after my friend died," he said. "He helped me a lot. Then when I was in college, I thought about getting a degree in psychology, so I took classes. But really, down deep inside, I was a fireman."

"So, was it worth it?" Bradley asked.

"Sure it paid off; you can really pick up chicks when you know this stuff."

Bradley laughed and it felt good. "Thanks, Mike."

"Hey, no problem," he replied. "Now let's get back home to Mary."

"Yeah, I wonder what she's been up to all day."

## Chapter Nineteen

"Are you sure we aren't going to be arrested for this?" Ian asked as he and Mary cut across the wide lawn of the high school and headed toward the door.

"No, of course not," she replied quietly. "Especially if we don't get caught."

"Oh, well, then, I'm feeling much better about the situation," he said.

She stopped for a moment and turned to him. "If someone questions us, just tell them you're from another country and didn't realize you couldn't go into a public building in the evening."

"Mary, I'm from Scotland, we can read English there," he said. "No one will believe me."

She shrugged. "Okay, well I guess our only option is to not get caught."

They pulled open the heavy door and quickly scanned the hallway. There was not a soul in sight. "Come on," she said. "The staircase is over here."

They hurried down the hallway and through the double doorway that opened to the stairs. Only the emergency lights glowed in the stairwell, casting shadows all around them.

"It's pretty creepy in here," Ian whispered.

Turning to him, Mary rolled her eyes. "What are you afraid of? Ghosts?"

He chuckled softly. "Good point."

They climbed the stairs to the second floor and peeked out through the doorway into the hall. They could hear voices coming from a well-lit room at one end. "We go this way," Mary whispered in a bad Vincent Price imitation, motioning in the opposite direction, "toward the dark end of the hall."

"Funny, Mary," Ian whispered back, "very funny."

Staying close to the lockers that lined the wall, they were able to stay in the shadows as they made their way to the chemistry lab. They approached the door and Ian stopped and slapped his forehead. "It's going to be locked," he whispered. "The school wouldn't allow the equipment to be out and about for anyone to take."

Mary shook her head. "Andy said the ghost unlocks the door because he doesn't want anyone to get caught in there again," she whispered. "Come on."

Sure enough, when Mary turned the knob, the door opened and they let themselves into the large darkened classroom. The window shades were all pulled down and only a few beams of illumination from the street light made their way in. Large dark lab tables flanked the perimeter of the room in two separate rows. Stainless steel shelving held beakers and Bunsen burners. A wall-sized large periodic table glimmered in the dark.

The door made a quiet snap when Mary shut it and Ian flinched. Chuckling, Mary came up beside him. "Jumpy professor?"

Her laughter stopped when she heard another voice, a deeper voice, join hers in amusement. "It's always the muscular types who are the real wimps."

"Would you like to put your money where your mouth is?" Ian asked, clearly offended.

Coach Thorne moved away from the back of the room, so the shadows only covered the top half of his body. "You can hear me?" he asked, astonished.

"Aye, and you could do with a lesson on manners," Ian grumbled.

"But...you can hear me," he said, wonder filling his voice.

Mary nodded. "Yes, and we can see you too, Coach Thorne."

"You know me? You know my name?"

"A friend of ours, Rosie Meriwether, sent us to you," Mary explained. "She told us you were a hero."

"Either a hero or an idiot," he said. "I guess the jury's still out."

"Aye, it is at that, Coach," Ian added, his arms folded over his chest.

The coach laughed. "Please, call me Charlie. And I admit I deserve that," he said. "I need to apologize. I was only making fun of you because I didn't think you could see me."

Ian's mouth grew into a small smile. "Well, I suppose I can't take offense at that," he said. "I would have probably done the same."

"I think I saw you at the hospital," Mary said. "Do you follow Louise around?"

He nodded. "I've watched her grow up, she's quite an amazing woman, don't you think?"

Mary nodded. "Yes, I agree. Do you remember the fire?"

Charlie stepped forward and Mary gasped. The skin on the right side of his face was melted and hanging off his skull. Where hair remained on the left side of his skull, it stood up in charred patches of black. One of his eyes was melted shut and the other lay in his eye socket, devoid of an eyelid or eyebrow. "Uh, yes, you could say I remember it well."

"Wow. The heat must have been intense," Ian said, moving toward the coach.

Charlie nodded. "Yeah, the explosion was intense," he said. "I'm sure the air was superheated because I don't remember anything until I woke up a ghost."

"What happened?" Mary asked.

"Wish I knew," he said. "We were mixing ammonium nitrate with water to create an endothermic reaction. Nothing like this should have happened."

"So you weren't using heat?" Ian asked.

"No, that's way too dangerous," Charlie said. "This should have been a safe experiment."

"Wait, why would you worry about heat?" Mary asked.

"Heating ammonium nitrate can cause a violent explosion," Ian said. "It can also react with certain kinds of combustible materials because it's a powerful oxidant."

Mary looked at Ian in disbelief.

"Ah, well, I was fairly good in organic chemistry," he confessed.

"Impressive," she replied and then turned to Charlie. "So, could this have just been an accident?"

"You know, I've been asking myself that too," he said. "I poured the ammonium nitrate into those test tubes myself. I kept all of the chemicals under lock and key. I just can't see how this could happen."

"Well, there's a reason you're still sticking around," Ian said. "And we'd like to help you figure that out."

"I know this is going to sound like a bad movie," Mary said. "But these are some of the things you need to consider. Did anyone have a grudge against you? Was there anyone who wanted you to look bad? It doesn't have to be murder, sometimes pranks can get out of control."

"I'll have to think about that," Charlie said. "I don't want to implicate anyone and ruin their life. They're only kids."

Mary smiled sadly. "Charlie, they're older than you are," she explained. "The explosion happened over forty years ago."

"Forty years?" he exclaimed. "I've been hanging around for forty years?"

"Aye," Ian said. "The trail's pretty cold, so we're going to need anything and everything you can remember."

They heard a noise in the hallway. "Ah, Speech Team is over," Mary said. "Charlie, we've got to go, but we'll be back to ask you some more questions."

Charlie shrugged. "I'll be here."

They slipped out the door and quietly made their way to the end of the hall. They could hear the students tease Mr. Connors, the Speech Team coach, and heard his bantering with them. Finally, the outside door closed and the high school was still.

"Ready?" Mary asked.

Ian nodded. "More than ready," he said. "High school scared me to death."

## Chapter Twenty

It was dark when Bradley pulled up in front of Mary's house. He and Mike made their way up to her front door and Bradley knocked while Mike stuck his head through the door to see if anyone was home.

"Rosie and Stanley are there," he said, pulling his head back. "And the kids are home, but there's no sign of Mary or Ian."

"Hmmm, well at least we know that she and Ian aren't going to be looking into anything dangerous," Bradley said.

Mike chuckled. "Yeah, right."

Bradley shot him a look of concern and was about to say something when the door opened. Rosie smiled up at Bradley. "Well, hello, Bradley," she said, "how nice to see you."

"Hello, Rosie, it's good to see you too," he replied. "Is Mary home?"

"Chief Alden," Andy cried, racing across the room. "Mary and Ian are breaking into the high school to catch a ghost."

"Oh, dear," Rosie sighed, biting her lower lip.

"Breaking in? As in breaking and entering?" Bradley asked Rosie.

"Well, not really breaking in," she said. "The door is unlocked, so they are merely entering, that's all. There's not a law against entering, is there?"

Bradley rolled his eyes. "Well, at least she has Ian with her."

"Oh, like that's going to help?" Mike teased.

Bradley felt a tug on his coat and looked down to find Maggie at his side. He smiled at her. "Hello, Maggie," he said, running his hand over her soft hair. "What can I do for you?"

"I miss Ian," she said. "Is he coming home soon?"

Bradley nodded. "He'd better be."

"Just got a call from Mary, she and Ian are on their way home," Stanley called from the kitchen.

"Stanley, don't come out here," Rosie yelled.

"What?" he asked.

He walked into the living room wearing a big white apron covered with flour. As a matter of fact, Bradley realized, he was totally covered in flour. Glancing around the room, Bradley saw the rest of the group also seemed to be wearing flour in the most unusual places. Maggie had flour on her nose and forehead. Andy's hair and shirt were coated. Rosie had a bit of flour on her cheek and on the back of her shirt, in the shape of handprints.

"What happened to you?" Bradley asked.

"Whoever puts their flour canister on a top shelf with the lid loose is asking for a mess, that's all I have to say," Stanley grumbled.

"The flour spilled all over Stanley," Maggie said. "He looks like a snowman."

"Yeah, it was so cool," Andy added. "There's flour everywhere in there. Me and Maggie got to have a food fight with Stanley. At least until Rosie told Stanley to stop."

"Yeah, then he kissed her and got flour on her cheek and her back," Maggie giggled.

"Sounds like a good time," he laughed.

"Well, it weren't a good time," Stanley said, a blush appearing on his wrinkled cheeks. "And now, some of us have to go to the store for more flour."

"While you're gone, the rest of us will sweep up your mess," Rosie said. "And don't forget milk. Mary's almost out."

"I won't forget," he said, letting himself out the door.

Bradley squatted down next to Maggie and brushed the flour off her nose and forehead. "A food fight, really?" he asked.

She grinned at him. "It was so fun," she said, her eyes widening. "My mom would never let us do something like that."

"Your mom is very smart," Bradley replied.

Andy came up next to him, a worried line furrowing his forehead. "Stanley said it was okay. Honest."

Bradley reached over and ruffled the boy's hair, a puff of flour escaping into the air. "Well, then, it must have been okay, because Stanley knows what he's doing," he said. "But we might want to clean it up before Mary and Ian get home."

Bradley shrugged off his coat and hung it in the closet. He rolled up the sleeves to his uniform shirt, exposing muscular forearms with a light dusting of dark hair. He smiled to the children. "Come on; let's clean the kitchen so Rosie can keep cooking."

"Oh, no, Bradley," Rosie fluttered. "I can't let you clean up this mess. You've worked all day. You probably haven't eaten dinner. You need to…"

Bradley looked over his shoulder at her, while he walked into the kitchen. "I'm fine, Rosie, real…ahhhhhh!"

Slipping on the slick floury kitchen floor, Bradley windmilled his arms as his feet flew out from under him and he landed on his back in a huge puff of white powder. He groaned softly.

"Bradley, are you okay?" Rosie gasped.

He nodded, raising his head and looking over at her. "Yeah. But you stay where you are, I don't want you to slip."

She giggled softly. "Oh, no, I don't want to end up on my backside either."

Bradley turned the other way to see both Maggie and Andy staring at him, their eyes wide and their faces worried. "If either of you laughs at me, you're in trouble," he said with a grin.

Andy slapped both hands over his mouth, but it was too late. A chortle escaped. Bradley rolled over and grabbed Andy around the waist, carefully wrestling him to the floor. "Now, you're in for it," he threatened, scooping up a handful of flour and stuffing it down Andy's shirt.

"This is war," Andy yelled, tossing fistfuls of flour into the air in the general direction of Bradley's head.

"Yeah, war," Maggie shouted, jumping on top of both of them.

Mary hurried up the front porch stairs. "I can't believe it's so late," she said, punching the security code into the lock. "I hope Bradley hasn't been here for long."

"Don't worry," Ian said. "Rosie's probably got the kids in bed, the cinnamon rolls made and the kitchen in perfect order."

"Yeah," Mary agreed, her hand on the doorknob. "And Bradley's probably relaxing with his feet up."

Mary stepped into the house and stared at the confusion in the kitchen. "Well," she said to Ian. "I was right about one thing; Bradley does have his feet up."

Bradley was lying on his back in the middle of the kitchen floor, his legs wrapped around Andy who was liberally sprinkling him with a dust pan filled with flour. Maggie appeared from the other side of the kitchen, poured a wooden spoon filled with flour on both of them, and danced back, keeping a step or two away from Bradley's outstretched arms.

"Get back here, you traitor," Bradley called. "You promised you would be on my side."

"I'm on my own side," Maggie giggled.

Mary closed the door with a slight thump and the room was immediately quiet.

"Uh, oh," Maggie whispered, hiding the spoon behind her back.

Bradley turned toward the door and Andy dumped the remaining flour onto the side of his face, covering him completely. He coughed and a cloud of flour surrounded his head.

"Ian, you're home," Maggie yelled, running across the room and throwing her flour-covered body against him.

He caught her up in his arms and looked down at her. "So, who do I have in me arms?" he asked. "It looks like a sugar cookie, not quite cooked."

She giggled. "It's me, Maggie," she explained. "Me and Andy are helping Chief Alden clean up the flour."

"And doing a remarkable job at it," Ian said, glancing over at Bradley. "Remind me never to hire you as a cleaning lady."

Bradley coughed again and blinked away the flour covering his eyes. "We seem to have had a little accident here," he explained.

Mary strolled across the room and looked at them. Both were covered with flour, their dark hair barely visible beneath the coating of white. Andy's face was a patchwork of freckles and flour. Bradley's an interesting combination of five o'clock shadow and white.

"So, um, what happened?" Mary asked.

"We was cleaning up the mess Stanley made," Andy explained, "and then Chief Alden slipped and fell on the floor. I was laughing so hard I spilled some flour on him."

Bradley coughed again, but this time it was directed at Andy.

Andy sighed. "Okay, I threw some flour at him," he admitted. "But he threw it back at me."

"He started it," Bradley said.

Mary bit the inside of her lip to keep from laughing and just shook her head. "I want you both to go out to the back porch and shake off as much flour as you can," she ordered.

"Yes, Mary," Andy said, trying to hid a grin.

Bradley stood up, showering the area with more flour. "Yes, Mary," Bradley repeated, but when she tried to turn away he caught her and gave her a big floury hug. "He *did* start it."

"You are such an idiot," she laughed, pushing him away and dusting herself off. "Go outside, now!"

"Do I have to go outside too, Mary?" Maggie asked.

Ian carried her over to the sink and stood her up on the counter. "Ach, no, I'll have you cleaned up in a trice," he said.

He pulled a feather duster out of the cabinet below the sink and held it in front of the little girl. "Are you ticklish by any chance?" he asked.

She giggled. "No," she lied.

He ran the duster across the top of her head and she laughed uncontrollably.

"I think you fibbed."

Mary grabbed a large bath towel and joined them at the sink. "I think this might do a better job," she said, wiping most of the flour off the little girl. "And now, my dear, I think it's time for a bath."

An hour later, the children were finally calm and in their beds. The kitchen was clean and cinnamon rolls were rising on the countertop.

Rosie and Stanley stood at the doorway ready to leave. Stanley's hair was still covered in flour and Rosie was trying hard to stifle her laughter. "Just put those rolls in the refrigerator once they're done rising," she said. "Then you can bake them in the morning."

"Thank you for making them and watching the children," Mary said.

"Oh, well, it was much more fun than I had imagined," Rosie giggled. "Stanley and I will come back tomorrow morning."

She leaned forward and whispered. "And you can tell me about you-know-what."

Nodding, Mary glanced over her shoulder to where Bradley was standing next to the sink, dressed only in his t-shirt, uniform pants and socks, shaking the flour out of his shirt and shoes. "Perfect, see you then."

She closed the door after them, leaned against the wall and sighed. "Well, that was fun," she said.

Bradley, his hair still peppered with flour, looked up from the shirt and sighed. "I really am sorry," he said. "I didn't mean for it to get so out of hand."

"Yeah, I watched the whole thing," Mike added. "He's the victim here all right. There were two of them and they took him by surprise. He didn't have a chance."

Ian chuckled. "Aye, they're a crafty team, alright," he said. "Posing as innocent children, and yet, they're probably wee bakers with an ax to grind or at the very least, some wheat to grind."

"Very funny," Bradley grumbled.

He rolled his shirt up in a ball and picked up his shoes. "Are you sure you don't need my help with the bathroom clean-up?" he asked. "I'm sure it's pretty bad."

"Mike and I are going up there just now," Ian said. "So, you two say your goodbyes and don't worry about us."

"I'm just supervising," Mike said, as he floated up the stairs behind Ian. "There's no way I want flour stuck to me. I'd look like a ghost."

Bradley chuckled and walked over to Mary. He put his hands against the wall behind her and slowly leaned toward her. "Is this okay?" he asked. "Any flashbacks?"

She lowered her head and then shook it.

He bent his head, trying to make eye contact, but she dropped her face even further.

"Mary, are you okay?" he asked. "Am I frightening you?"

A chortle escaped her lips and he watched her shoulders shake in silent laughter. She finally lifted her head; tears were streaming down her face which was red from trying to hold back her amusement. She lifted her hand to her mouth. "I'm so sorry," she giggled. "I was really trying…"

He lifted her chin with his finger. "Trying to do what? Resist my half-baked personality?"

She giggled, "I am trying to watch my carb intake."

He placed a lingering kiss on her jawline. "So, the Pillsbury Dough Boy doesn't turn you on?" he asked.

She shuddered with delight. "Well," she exclaimed, clearing her throat. "He never did in the past."

He grinned and kissed her again. "Let's see if I can't just help you change your mind about baked goods."

She slipped her arms around his neck and threaded her fingers into his hair, releasing a small cascade of flour onto both of them. "I just decided that I really love carbs."

He smiled down at her, his eyelids half closed, his smile lazy. "Well, that's a bonus for both of us," he whispered, before he leaned down and crushed his mouth against hers.

# Chapter Twenty-one

The scent of freshly baked cinnamon rolls greeted Ian as he strolled down the stairs the next morning. He looked into the kitchen and found Mary scooping the rolls onto a platter and humming softly to herself, her face aglow.

"So, up early this morning, I see," he said, sauntering over to the counter and helping himself to a roll.

"I had a great night's sleep," she replied. "Can't recall when I've slept as well."

"Aye, there's naught like a bit of smooching and hugging to chase the goblins away, I always say," he said, winking at her.

Mary blushed. "Shut up and eat your roll," she ordered.

Grinning, he took a big bite and closed his eyes in ecstasy. "Ah, the woman is a saint," he moaned, "that's all I have to say."

Mary grinned. "Yes, she is and she's a pretty good cook too."

Ian chuckled. "Aye, that she is," he said, placing his elbows on the counter and smiling up at Mary. "And so, darling, aside from the humming and the beaming, how are you really feeling this morning?"

Pulling a couple of saucers and some cups from the cabinet and placing them on the counter, she took a few moments before answering him. "Last night…when Bradley kissed me…I felt like things had returned to normal," she said slowly. "In the back of my mind I was a little worried I'd start getting flashbacks. But once we got…going." She blushed. "I kind of…I didn't…"

"You were a little too preoccupied to think about the back of your mind?" Ian suggested.

She nodded and rolled her eyes. "Yes, exactly," she said. "And please stop grinning at me."

He pushed himself off the counter and walked around it to stand next to her. "I'm grinning because your happiness is contagious," he said. "There's naught like a lass in love. But you need to realize it doesn't mean everything's fine about you."

She nodded. "I know," she said. "Small steps."

"Aye," he agreed. "Small steps."

Just then they heard a noise from upstairs. "Speaking of small steps," Ian said. "I do believe we are going to be invaded."

Maggie and Andy hurtled down the stairs. "I smell cinnamon rolls," Andy announced. "And I'm hungry as a bear."

"Me too," Maggie added. "A polar bear."

"A polar bear?" Ian asked.

"'Cause it's snowy outside," Maggie explained.

"Duh," Mary whispered to Ian, and then in a normal voice, she added, "So, who's ready for cinnamon rolls and milk?"

"Did you see the ghost at the high school?" Andy asked between bites.

"Aye, we did," Ian said. "Although I have to say Mary was a wee bit frightened. Of course, I protected her."

Maggie smiled at Ian. "I wouldn't be afraid of ghosts," she said, wiping some frosting from her mouth. "I like ghosts."

Andy rolled his eyes. "I bet you'd scream your head off if you saw one," he said.

"Would not," she replied.

"Would too."

"Would not."

Mary looked over at Ian and grinned. "See what you started."

"Did not," he replied.

"Did so."

"Did not."

"Everyone just shut up!" Mike roared, appearing next to the counter in the kitchen. "You're making enough noise to wake the dead and I should know!"

"Would too," Andy said with a triumphant smile, and then he looked around the room. "What?"

Mary and Ian stood in stunned silence and watched Maggie shyly smile at Mike.

"Andy, why don't you go up and brush your teeth?" Mary said. "I'll help Maggie with hers down here."

Andy stuffed the last bit of roll into his mouth and darted up the stairs.

Ian slid into Andy's chair and turned to Maggie. "So, darling, is there a special reason you're not afraid of ghosts?" he asked.

She giggled softly and quickly glanced at Mike and then away again. "No."

"The jigs up sweetheart," Mike said in his best Bogart impression. "They can see me too."

Maggie's eyes went wide with wonder. "Really, you can see Fireman Mike?" she asked.

Kneeling down in front of her chair, Mary faced the little girl. "Yes, we can," she said. "But how did you know his name was Mike?"

"He's my guardian angel," she said with a radiant smile. "He protects me while I sleep so I don't have to be afraid when Mommy and Daddy aren't here."

Mike shrugged. "She needed a drink of water the other night and it was dark in her room," he explained. "I figured since I was up…"

Mary smiled at him. "That was very sweet of you," she said. "You make a good guardian angel."

Turning back to Maggie, she said, "So, sweetheart, about Fireman Mike, I think it's probably smart to keep him our secret."

Maggie sighed and nodded. "I know. Some people just don't know how to handle ghosts," she said.

Ian leaned over and kissed her forehead. "Aye, darling, most people don't know how to handle ghosts, but I can see you do. Perhaps when you've grown a bit you can come and work for me."

"After we're married?" she asked.

He chuckled, "Aye, after we're married."

Mary stood up and offered her hand to Maggie. "Come on; let's go get your teeth brushed before the bus comes."

Ten minutes later, the house was finally quiet again. Maggie and Andy had been successfully placed on the bus with their backpacks and lunches. Maggie's secretive wave at Mike convinced Mary and Ian that she would not be sent to the school psychologist for mentioning she could see dead people.

"Was that crazy or what?" Ian asked, closing the door as the bus pulled away from the curb.

"Well, I can tell you one thing," Mike said. "I'm not the first ghost she's seen."

"What?" Mary exclaimed, quickly turning toward him, her hands filled with plates and cups. "Why would you say that?"

"Because when she saw me hovering next to the bed she merely said, 'Oh, hello,' rather than 'AHHHHHHHHHHH.'"

"Aye, that would be a dead giveaway," Ian said. "No offense intended."

Mike chuckled. "None taken."

Shaking her head, Mary slipped the dishes into the sink and started loading the dishwasher. "I'm not sure this is healthy for her," she said. "In the real world most little girls her age play with Barbies, not dead people."

"Of course it's healthy," Ian said, popping another piece of cinnamon roll into his mouth. "And it's bloody fortuitous. She won't live her life thinking she's nuts. She'll understand that other people have her special gift and she'll have, in a way, a support group."

Shrugging, Mike floated toward Mary. "He has a point. I think it's great she's not afraid of me," he said. "But she also needs to learn that not all spirits are friendly Fireman Mike. So, I agree, it's a good thing."

Mary closed the dishwasher and pressed the button to get it started. "Okay, maybe you're right," she said. "But I'm going to speak with her mother about it, just so she knows."

"That's a good idea," Ian said. "Research shows that this kind of gift is passed down through bloodlines. Perhaps Katie is able to see ghosts too."

"Well, she's always seemed open to what I do," Mary agreed. "Perhaps she does."

"In the meantime," Ian said. "We've got a mystery to solve. How do we go about getting access to the high school after hours?"

"I'll call Bradley at the office," Mary said, walking over to the table and reaching for her cell. "I'm sure he'll be able to…"

"Bradley's not in the office today," Mike said, hesitating for a moment.

"Where is he?" Mary asked. "Mike, is something wrong?"

"They're exhuming Jeannine's body today," he replied. "He's gone into Chicago to be there."

Mary sat down on a chair and shook her head. "Oh, poor Bradley," she whispered. "He shouldn't have to do this by himself."

"He won't be by himself," Mike said. "He went to see Jeannine's parents yesterday. They're going to meet him there."

"I'm so glad," she said. "They all need closure."

"He's was going to tell you," Mike said. "But I think he got distracted."

"Aye, and by more than just a flour war," Ian teased.

Mary sent him a warning glance and then turned back to Mike. "Are you going to be with him?"

"Yeah, I thought I'd hang with him, just in case," he said.

"Thanks, and if you think…"

"Yeah, if he needs you, I'll let you know," Mike agreed before fading away.

"Well, now we have to find another way into that school," Ian said.

# *Chapter Twenty-two*

The sun shone brightly, the sky was brilliant blue, but the wind chill brought the temperature down to the mid-teens. Bradley stood at the edge of the cemetery, the wind whipping his overcoat, as he watched the back hoe dig up the grave that stood beneath the marker with Beverly Copper's name inscribed upon it.

"It should be raining," Mike said softly, appearing next to him. "It should be overcast and there should be no sun in the sky."

Bradley nodded and dug his hands further into the pockets of his coat as another strong wind buffeted his body. "No, I think this is better," he replied, his voice despondent. "She loved the rain. She loved a good thunderstorm. I think it's much better to have it bitterly cold and harsh today. It suits the event."

"Got it," the young man driving the back hoe yelled out.

A group of men who had been standing behind a small mausoleum to deflect the wind made their way to the gravesite. One of the men looked their way and waved to Bradley.

"Who's that?" Mike asked.

"Mary's brother, Sean, he's leading the investigation."

"Good guy?"

"Yeah. Yeah, he is."

Bradley walked over to the gravesite. Sean and another man, a very large man with blond hair and bright blue eyes, motioned him over. "Bradley, this in Bernie Wojchichowski, Cook County Coroner. Bernie, this is Police Chief Bradley Alden."

"Yeah? We met already, on the phone," he said, offering a beefy hand for a shake. "You was working with little O'Reilly."

Suddenly it dawned on Bradley who he was meeting. "Oh, you're the guy with the nephew," he said.

"Yeah, and if you don't do right by my little Mary, me and my nephew are on the next train to Freeport."

"Freeport doesn't have a train," Sean said.

"Okay, well, we'll get there, all right," he said. "And my nephew will carry her off whether she likes it or not."

"She'll kick his ass," Sean commented mildly.

Bernie sighed. "Yeah, you're right, she would."

He turned to Bradley. "You just do good by her, got it?"

Bradley felt his smile beginning to melt his frozen features. "Yeah, I got it."

"So, how come you're here?" Bernie asked.

"Jeannine, the body in the grave, she's Bradley's wife," Sean explained before Bradley could say a word.

"Oh, man, that's tough," Bernie said, clapping a solid grip on Bradley's shoulder and moving him toward the grave. "Well, let's get this over to my office and then we can take a look."

"But her parents," Bradley said.

"Yeah, we know they're on their way," Bernie said. "But I always like to take a look at stuff before I let the family look. You get what I'm saying?"

Bradley nodded. "Yeah, of course, that makes sense," he said, wondering what kind of horrors Bernie had encountered to make him so cautious.

"It ain't always bad stuff," he reassured Bradley. "It's just, you know, little stuff, like the skull rolling down next to the feet. Stuff like that freaks people out."

Bradley cleared his throat, picturing a grinning skull lodged between a corpse's feet. "Yeah, I could see how that might upset someone."

Bernie stopped walking and looked intently at Bradley. "You want to be here or do you want to wait a ways back?" he asked. "Ain't no shame in waiting. This ain't the job; this here's your wife."

Shaking his head, Bradley stepped forward. "No, I have to be here."

"Yeah, I get that," Bernie said.

The other men from the group had attached thick metal cable to the outside of the concrete burial vault and quickly climbed out of the grave. The back hoe was facing the opposite direction, where a small crane was attached. The operator lowered a thick hook and the men guided it to where the cables joined above the vault. Once it was secure, the men signaled the operator and the top of the vault was raised from the earth and slowly lowered onto the ground near the grave.

Bradley peered down into the grave and saw the oak coffin lying inside the remainder of the vault. *This is where she's been laying for eight long years,* he thought and his stomach twisted.

A strong arm clamped around his shoulders and he looked over to see Sean standing next to him. "You know better than I do that this is just a resting place for bones," Sean whispered. "Jeannine was never in here, just her shell. Her spirit was always free."

Bradley took a deep shuddering breath; he hadn't realized there were tears on his face. "I know," he said, "but thanks for reminding me."

Bradley stepped out of the way as the men attached cables to the outside of the casket and lifted it out of the earth. Bradley, Sean, Bernie and several others moved forward and took hold of the casket. The cables were released and the men reverently carried the casket to the back of a waiting hearse. In a matter of minutes, Bradley was following it back to the coroner's office.

# Chapter Twenty-three

"So you actually spoke with him?" Rosie asked Mary and Ian, her tea cup nervously clattering against the saucer.

"Yes, we did," Mary said. "And he seemed like a very nice man."

"Did he know why he's still there?" she asked.

"We really didn't have enough time to get into details," Ian confided. "We're hoping to find a way to get back into the school."

Rosie bent over, placed her cup on the coffee table. "And this time it must be honestly," she said. "I couldn't face disappointing Bradley again."

Mary smiled. "Well, of course we need to do it honestly. So, who do we know that can let us in?"

Suddenly Rosie sat up and smiled widely. "Why, of course, how silly of me."

"How silly of you what?" Ian asked.

"Why, I went to school with the superintendent of schools," she said. "Wally Gormley. But he likes to be called Walter now."

"And how would you go about having Walter get us a key to the school?" Ian asked.

Rosie thought for a moment. "I could tell him you're a professor from a university in Scotland," she announced with delight.

"Aye, I can see how he might be believing that," Ian said with a smirk. "And what would I want to be doing tooling around the high school at night."

She thought for another moment. "You're sensitive to light, so you need to do your work at night, when no one is there?"

He shook his head. "I sound like a Scottish vampire, I don't think he'd let me wander the halls with that kind of a reason."

"Well, vampires are all the rage these days," Rosie replied.

"But not something the superintendent would sanction in the high school," Mary added. "What other reason would someone want to study a building when no one is occupying it?"

"Why don't I tell him that you're researching radon gas exposure?" she said slowly. "And you can't get correct readings when the students are walking around and the doors are opening and closing."

"That's a good idea, Rosie," Mary said.

"It is?" Rosie asked.

"It is?" Ian asked.

"Yes, it is," Mary replied with a smile. "We're considered a Zone One for radon, which means we have the highest potential for it. A study like that would make sense."

"Well, Rosie, apparently that was brilliant," Ian said, lifting his cup of tea up to toast her. "Would you like me to go with you when you meet with him? I could say a couple of things in Scottish."

Rosie considered Ian's words for a moment. "No, no, I think I should go and meet with Wally all by myself at first. We used to be an item, and I don't know how he'll react if he were to see me with such a young and handsome fellow."

"Ach, but you're a flatterer, you are."

She stood up and smiled at Ian. "You start researching radon, just in case he wants to talk to you about the study," she said. "We have to be believable."

"Yes, ma'am," Ian said.

Rosie slipped her coat on and walked over to Mary and gave her a hug. "Now, you just leave it to me," she said. "I'll handle this perfectly."

"Thank you, Rosie," she said. "And, just to be on the safe side, don't bring my name up. I seem to be getting a bit of a reputation in town. It might be better if people aren't reminded that I can see ghosts."

"Of course, that makes perfect sense," she said. "Besides, it will never come up. All we want to do is talk about radon."

Fifteen minutes later, Rosie was standing in front of the superintendent's assistant's desk. A trim woman with dark hair pulled back in an efficient bun, she wore a slim navy blue skirt, white blouse and sensible shoes.

"Hello, I'd like to see Wally, I mean Walter Gormley, please," Rosie said to the woman with a friendly smile.

"Do you have an appointment?" the woman asked coldly.

Rosie shook her head. "Oh, no, this is a spur of the moment visit," she said. "We're old friends."

"The superintendent rarely has time for visits from old friends," the assistant said. "He has a very busy schedule."

Rosie smiled at the woman and said, "Why don't you ask him and let him make the decision? My name is Rosie Meriwether."

The woman sniffed loudly, and then disappeared into the room behind her desk. After a moment the door was opened. "Let her in, let her in," Wally insisted, as he moved his rather large girth around his desk and greeted Rosie.

"Rosie Meriwether, it seems like forever," he said, clasping her delicate hands in his flaccid damp one.

Rosie smiled while cringing inwardly. "Wally, I mean Walter, it's wonderful to see you too," she echoed. "It's just been too long. And look, you haven't changed at all."

Walter beamed at her through myopically thick glasses. "Why thank you, dear, and may I say the same about you."

She tittered over the compliment and he smiled with delight.

"Well, come in and have a seat in my office," he invited. "And tell me what it is I can do for you."

He leaned a little closer. "I am a man with a great deal of influence now."

Rosie smiled at him. "Oh, Walter, you were always a man with influence in my book."

He led her to a chair and then squeezed back behind his desk and sank down. Rolling his chair forward to the desk, he placed his sagging elbows on it and templed his fingers. "Your wish, dear, is my command."

She leaned slightly forward in her chair, her proper form presenting perfect posture and lady-like demeanor. "I have a friend, actually the son of a friend, who is a college professor from Scotland, University of Edinburgh," she began.

"Good school, fine school," he harrumphed.

She nodded. "Oh, yes, it is," she agreed. "He is in the States studying, er, radon gas. Yes, that's right. Radon gas in public schools."

"Oh, is that a concern?"

Rosie nodded. "Oh, yes, Stephenson County is Level One in radon probability," she said. "But I'm sure you knew that."

"Well, yes, of course I did," Walter said, his cascading chins wobbling in agreement. "Go on, please."

"Well, he would like to study one of our schools," she said. "Which is very exciting, don't you think, having one of our schools studied in a national, er, study?"

"Yes, I think that could be beneficial."

"Especially for grant money," Rosie added.

One eyebrow soared into his forehead. "Grant money?"

"Oh, yes," she said eagerly, and then she stopped and bit her lower lip. "I mean, that's a possibility, wouldn't you think?"

"Yes. Yes, that could be good for us."

"So, he would like to study the high school, at night, and would need access to go inside, at night, and, er, study it," she concluded with a smile.

"But the high school has already been studied for radon," Walter said, cocking his head slightly so he resembled a hairless grizzly bear. "Didn't he know that?"

"Oh, dear," Rosie said nervously. "This isn't working the way I thought it would."

Walter moved his hands so they clasped the front of his desk and leaned forward. "I remember that you used to be rather good at telling tales, Rosie," he said, his jowls flattening angrily. "Are you lying to me?"

Rosie thought quickly, there had to be a way to fix this situation.

"Yes, I am lying to you," she said. "He's not studying radon, he's studying ghosts."

Walter pushed his hands against the desk and his chair rolled backward into the bookcase. "Ghosts?" he said. "What the hell are you talking about, Rosie?"

She paused for a moment, she wasn't supposed to tell about Mary, but she couldn't remember if she could tell about Ian. Perhaps she should only tell a little about Ian.

"Do you have the Internet?" she asked.

Walter nodded.

"Google the name Professor Ian MacDougal," she requested, "Edinburgh University."

He typed into the search engine and waited for a moment.

"Criminology with an emphasis on Paranormal Phenomena and Criminalistics?" he read. "What kind of bunk is that?"

"Oh, no, he's quite renowned," she explained. "Which is why I called him here. I only wanted the best for Coach Thorne."

Walter's eyes widened. "Coach Thorne?" he gasped. "What the hell are you talking about?"

Rosie moved her chair up next to the front of the desk and leaned forward. She placed her hand on Walter's arm and met his eyes. "Walter, I need to tell you something. Something I've kept a secret for most of my life. Walter, I see dead people."

# Chapter Twenty-four

Bradley was grateful to the men who helped him carry Jeannine's casket from the hearse to the lab at the coroner's office. They did their job with reverence and respect, speaking in low voices and treating the casket with care. When they finally placed it on the low platform, they turned and shook Bradley's hand, offering him their condolences.

Sean waited until they left and put his hand on Bradley's shoulder. "You ready?"

Bradley nodded.

Sean and Bernie stepped forward, each holding a medium-sized Allen wrench-like key. They walked to either side of the casket, inserted the keys and turned them, unlocking the lid. Bradley heard the thump signaling the lid's release and took a deep breath.

Bernie moved back. "You can open it," he said. "We can give you a minute."

Bradley took a few steps forward and ran his hand along the smooth finish of the oak casket. He slipped his fingers around a bronzed handle on the top and on the bottom of the casket and deliberately pushed up. A wave of putrid air washed over him and he gagged.

"Sorry, forgot to tell you," Bernie said. "That first whiff can be powerful."

Bradley pushed past the smell and leaned over the casket. It was hard to believe the collection of whitened bones lying on a cushion of stained white was actually Jeannine. He shook his head. It was like staring down at something from a museum, not his wife.

He studied her, from the top of her skull across the remnants of the clothing she'd been buried in to the tiny bones scattered around the slippers at the base of the casket. Then he noticed her hand. It lay on top of her ribcage, as if her hands had been folded over her chest in repose. And on the third bone of her left hand, a golden ring still sparkled.

He reached out and placed his hand over hers.

"I found your body, Jeannine," he whispered. "You're not lost anymore."

The intercom crackled behind him. "Bernie, there's a Mr. and Mrs. Whitley here to see you."

Bradley turned. "Jeannine's parents," he explained.

Bernie walked over to the desk and pressed the black button on the intercom. "Yeah, Suzie, go ahead and send them down. I'll meet them at the door."

He looked at Bradley. "So, is it your wife?"

"Yeah, she's still got her wedding ring on."

"Okay, I can let her folks see her," he said. "But I then I need some time to compare dental records and see if I can get anything on toxicology."

"But she's been dead eight years," Sean said.

"Yeah, I know," Bernie countered. "But we want to put this jerk away for a long time, right? And if some of her hair still carries traces of the stuff he was giving her, we have more evidence against him."

"Hair, huh?" Sean asked.

"Yeah, it's a long shot, considering how old the samples are," he said with a shrug. "But, hell, I'm willing to give it a shot."

"I appreciate it, Bernie," Bradley said.

"Hey, if it was someone from my family, you'd do the same."

Bradley met his eyes. "Yes, I would," he said. "But I pray it never is."

A soft knock on the office door halted their conversation.

"Let me talk to them first," Bernie said, turning and walking over to the door.

"Mr. and Mrs. Whitley, I'm Bernie Wojchichowski, Cook County Coroner," he said. "I'm sorry for your loss."

"Thank you," Joyce said, her voice trembling. "Have you found her?"

Bernie nodded. "Yes, we were able to exhume her body this morning," he said. "But before you go over and look at her, I just want to talk to you for a few minutes. Is that okay with you?"

They nodded and Bernie led them into the room. Bradley came forward and hugged them both. Joyce clasped his hand tightly and kept hold of it while Bernie led them across the room to his desk. Joyce froze for a moment when she saw the casket lying on the raised platform. Bill put his arm around her shoulders and guided her forward, although her gaze never left the casket.

"Is that…?" she stammered, tears filling her eyes.

Bradley nodded. "Yes, that's Jeannine."

He and Bill helped her into a chair and sat on either side of her, offering her comfort. She released Bradley's hand and searched in her purse for a handkerchief, blotting the moisture from her eyes. "I'm fine," she said. "Please continue with your talk."

Bernie sat on the edge of the desk in front of them. "Are you religious people?" Bernie asked.

They both nodded at him and he smiled. "Good, because that always makes this conversation easier."

He reached back and opened one of the drawers, pulled out a white cotton glove and put it on his hand. "Okay, so this is not a conversation that has been sanctioned by the City of Chicago or Cook County," he said. "This is a conversation between people, religious people, about death and stuff you learn when you're a coroner. Understand?"

Once again, they nodded.

Bernie raised his gloved hand and wiggled his fingers. "What you see here is a glove moving, right?" he looked at Bradley.

"Right," Bradley said.

"Wrong," Bernie replied. "What you got here is my hand moving, but it's covered by a glove, so you think it's the glove moving."

He pulled the glove off his hand and threw it up in the air. The glove dropped down onto the top of the desk. "Without my hand, the glove looks like it did before, but there ain't no movement, there ain't no life and there ain't no Wojchichowski charm attached to it. It's just a shell."

He stood up and walked over to the casket. "What we got in here is a glove," he said. "It's a glove that's been buried in the ground for eight years, so Mother Nature took her toll. But you gotta remember that what you are going to see, ain't your daughter. She's left that glove eight years ago."

"And what you need to remember is she's still alive, but she's in another place," he said, "a better place. And I personally think she probably looks like when her glove was fresh and new, nothing like what you're going to see in that casket. Do you understand what I'm saying?"

Joyce nodded and placed her hand on top of her husband's hand. "Yes," she said. "Thank you."

They stood and made their way to the casket, Bill's arm around Joyce's waist. They stopped together, leaned forward and looked at the remains. Joyce gasped, turned her head into her husband's shoulder and wept. He held her tightly, his eyes still on the skeleton before them.

"You're right," he said to Bernie. "Our daughter is already home with her Father. Thank you for reminding us."

"Bill, can I...?" Bradley paused, unsure of what to do.

"I think Joyce and I need some time together to let this all sink in," he said. "Thank you for finding her, Bradley. We'll see you on Saturday."

He turned slowly and guided his wife out of the room.

# *Chapter Twenty-five*

Walter sat back in his chair. "You see dead people?" he asked, disbelief showing clearly in his face.

"Well, I know it sounds strange," she agreed with a tentative smile. "But I can see and talk to ghosts. So, that's why Ian got in touch with me. I've, er, I've been useful in some police investigations and the Chicago Police Department mentioned my name."

"Rosie, you have to admit this takes a little getting used to," he admitted.

"Well, of course it does," she agreed. "And believe me; it took a little getting used to on my part."

"There are a lot of ghost stories in Freeport," Walter said. "Why the high school?"

"Well, if Coach Thorne is still around, I'd like to help him move on," she explained. "He saved my life. He saved your life. The least we can do is save his, er, afterlife."

Walter drummed his fingers on his desk. "So you don't know if Coach Thorne is still around…as a ghost."

Rosie decided Wally didn't need to know Mary and Ian had already gotten into the school. "No, I don't know for sure," she said. "But there are still stories about the high school being haunted, and I thought we could start there."

Shaking his head, Walter sat back comfortably in his chair. "Well, Rosie, as much as I'd like to help you, you know I have to answer to the school board," he said pretentiously. "Often my hands are tied and I'm afraid in this case…"

Rosie sighed. "Oh, well, don't worry about it, Walter," she said, interrupting him. "Once Bradley gets back into town, I'm sure…"

"Bradley," Walter said, sitting up straight in his chair.

"Yes, Bradley, you know, Chief Alden," Rosie said. "Once Police Chief Alden gets back in town, I'm sure he'll be interested…"

"No, no, no," Walter interrupted eagerly. "We don't want to bother the police chief with something like this. He's a busy, busy man. I'm sure there won't be a problem for you to get access to the high school in the evenings."

Rosie clapped her hands. "Oh, really? That would be just wonderful."

"I'll just have my secretary get you a pass key to the high school," he said, pressing his intercom and repeating the request to his secretary. "But I do have a request."

"Well, of course," Rosie said. "What would you like?"

"Well, I'm a fan of Coach Thorne, he was such a hero," he said. "I would consider it a personal favor if you could keep me updated on the status of your investigation."

"Oh, of course," Rosie agreed. "I'm sure that won't be a problem."

"Wonderful," he said. "Call me once you have any information and I'll meet with you to go over it."

The office door opened and his secretary came in with the key. Rosie stood, took the key and thanked her. She turned to Walter and offered him her hand. "Thank you so much," she said. "I know we are both going to be so surprised with the outcome of this research."

He took her hand and offered her a weak handshake. "You have no idea, Rosie," he said. "No idea at all."

Once she left the room, he pressed the button on the intercom. "Gladys, hold all my calls for the next thirty minutes," he ordered.

Pulling one of his drawers open, he pulled out a bottle of Scotch and a glass tumbler. His hands shook as he unscrewed the top of the bottle and poured a generous amount of the amber liquid into the glass. He placed the open bottle next to the phone, lifted the glass and took a large gulp. He winced at the burn in his throat, but immediately lifted the glass and drank deeply again. Finally, he lifted the handset on his phone and dialed a number. He patted his forehead with a tissue while he waited for the call to be answered.

"This is Walter," he said without any greeting. "We've got to get together and quick. We've got trouble."

## Chapter Twenty-six

Bradley stared at the door that had just closed behind Jeannine's parents.

"Damn."

"Yeah, but the ones you gotta worry about are the ones that ain't crying when they leave here," Bernie said. "Those two, it's gonna take a while, but they're going to be fine."

Bradley took a deep breath. "Okay, so what do you still need from me?" he asked.

"Nothing," Bernie said, patting Bradley on the back. "Except for you to get the hell out of my office so I can get some work done."

Bradley smiled. "Yeah, okay, I can do that," he said. "Thanks Bernie."

"Hey Bernie, we're going to leave Bradley's cruiser in the lot, if that's okay with you," Sean said. "I got to bring him over to meet Pete O'Bryan."

"Yeah, really? You got Pete to help him?" Bernie said, nodding his head, obviously impressed. "That'll be good. And, if that don't work, I got this other nephew…"

Sean pushed Bradley toward the door. "It'll work," he called behind him. "But thanks anyway Bernie."

The door swung shut behind them and Bradley turned to Sean. "Who's Pete O'Bryan and why am I going to meet with him?"

"Pete's one of the best lawyers in the city," Sean said. "He and I went to college together, we both played football. He was the quarterback and I was the left tackle, protecting his butt during every game. He owes me a couple, so I called one in."

Bradley stopped in the middle of the hallway. "Wait a minute," he said, "one of the best lawyers in the city? I appreciate the favor, Sean, and you know I'm going to do everything in my power to find my little girl. But I've got to be realistic too. I don't have that kind of money."

"Bradley, when I said Pete owed me, I meant it. No charge. He's doing this pro bono."

Bradley was dumbfounded. "What? Why?"

"I told him my future brother-in-law was looking for his little girl," Sean explained over his shoulder as he walked down the hall. "It's an early wedding gift."

Rushing after him, Bradley grabbed his shoulder. "Wait a minute," he said.

"What, you change your mind?"

"No, of course not. But I haven't even asked her yet."

"Not while she was awake, anyway," Sean teased, continuing down the hall.

"I haven't asked your dad for permission," Bradley countered, hurrying after him.

"Yeah, we're having breakfast with them in the morning," Sean said. "You're spending the night at my place."

"Dammit, you're not my big brother," Bradley said, grabbing hold of the door before Sean could exit.

Sean looked at him and grinned. "Not yet," he said. "But soon."

An hour later they were escorted into a posh private waiting room with windows that overlooked Lake Michigan. The floor was polished oak and the furniture was dark brown leather and mahogany.

"Nice digs," Sean said, sinking into one of the chairs. "But it would be better if it had a pool table."

"I'll take that into advisement," said the man who entered the room from a door on the other side of the room.

Bradley looked over and was surprised to see that the robust voice came from a man who was sitting in a wheelchair. His upper body was strong and well-developed, but the rest of his body, from his waist down was covered by a blanket. He wheeled over to Bradley and extended his hand; even in the wheelchair he seemed tall. "Hi, I'm Pete," he said, his smile was wide and his blue eyes were sharp and intelligent. "Sean told me a little about your situation."

Bradley shook his hand, impressed by the strong grip. "I'm grateful you're willing to help me."

"Hey, if you're a part of Sean's family, you're part of my family too," he said. "Why don't you sit down? It's breaking my neck looking up at you."

Bradley was immediately taken aback; he glanced around for a chair. "Oh, I'm so…"

"Listen, Pete, take it easy on the guy," Sean said. "He's actually one of those polite and caring types."

Pete laughed. "Sorry, I have a weird sense of humor," he admitted. "Come on; let's go into my office where we can talk."

They followed Pete back through the door he used to come in and entered a beautifully furnished office that was obviously designed for Pete's wheelchair. Bradley looked around and noted the trophies on the shelves testifying to Pete's athletic accomplishments in the past. A framed degree from an Ivy League Law School hung on the wall behind his desk. Pete wheeled behind a large wooden desk and tapped a button. A computer monitor raised out of the middle of the desk.

"Don't you just love technology?" he asked with a grin. "Now, let's get started."

Three hours later, Bradley's head was spinning. He had a list of things he needed to document and he was in awe of the attention to detail and knowledge Pete possessed. He could actually feel hope burning in his chest, if anyone was going to be able to cut through the red tape and sealed adoption records, it would be Pete.

He stood up, leaned over the desk and extended his hand to Pete. "Thank you," he said earnestly. "I'm grateful for what you're doing."

Pete shook his hand. "Hey, it's the least I can do for someone in the O'Reilly clan."

"Well, I'm not part of the clan yet," he admitted.

"Yeah, he's going to talk to Dad tomorrow and get his permission," Sean added.

"Good luck, Bradley," Pete said. "I wouldn't want to be in your shoes."

"Thanks…I think," Bradley said. "Hey, do you want to be there? Maybe you could represent me."

Pete laughed. "Oh, no, I stay out of family matters like these."

Bradley sighed. "I knew you were a smart man."

Sean laughed. "Hey, don't worry; I've got your back. Besides, I invited Art and Tom to be there too."

"The twins?" Pete asked. "Most guys only have to face the father, not all the brothers too."

Sean grinned. "He can take it," he said. "Besides, Ma likes him."

Pete nodded. "With Maggie O'Reilly on your side, you don't need a thing more."

Bradley shook his head. "So why do I feel like I'm going to my own execution?"

## Chapter Twenty-seven

"I'm back," Rosie sang as she danced through Mary's front doorway.

Stanley rose from Mary's couch and walked over to meet her. "Why didn't you tell me you was going to meet with Wally?" Stanley said. "I woulda gone with you."

"Well, Stanley, it just wouldn't have worked as well," she explained.

Stanley squinted his eyes and stared at her. "Was you using your womanly wiles on that poor man?"

Rosie blushed. "No. Well, maybe a little. But it was for a good cause. I got the key."

Ian clapped his hands. "Good for you, Rosie," he said. "Mission accomplished."

Mary, her arms full of laundry, came walking down the stairs. "What's going on?"

"Rosie got her man and got the key," Ian said.

"She got the key alrighty," Stanley said. "But the only man she's getting around here is me."

Rosie reached up and placed a kiss on Stanley's cheek. "You're the only man I want to get," she said, tenderly patting his cheek.

"So, do I have to wear a radon suit or something like that?" Ian asked.

She shook her head. "Oh, no, the school was already tested for radon," she said. "So that idea didn't work at all."

"Oh, sorry, Rosie," Mary said. "I thought that was a sure-fire winner."

Shaking her head, Rosie slipped off her coat and hung it over the back of the chair. "Well, actually, the funny thing is...," she paused for a moment, lowered her head and bit her lower lip. "The thing is, I couldn't think of anything else, so I told him the truth."

Mary dropped the laundry. "What truth?" she asked.

"I told him to do a Google search on Ian," she said. "And he saw that he was a professor."

"And that my specialty is paranormal phenomena and criminalistics," Ian added.

"Yes," Rosie admitted and then turned to Mary. "But I didn't tell him about you. So, this will work perfectly."

Stanley put his hands on his hips. "Sounds like you ain't telling us everything, girlie," he said. "What else?"

Rosie sighed deeply. "Well, I may have led him to believe that I..." she hesitated.

"That you..." Mary encouraged.

"That I can see ghosts."

Stanley strode up next to Rosie. "You told him you could see ghosts?" he asked, his arms gesticulating in every direction. "You know what you did? You realize what you did? You placed yourself in danger. That's what you did."

Rosie took a deep breath and faced Stanley. She pointed her finger at him. "Yes, I did," she said. "I put myself in a little danger, and do you know why?"

"Yeah, I want to know."

She put her finger on his chest and pushed, knocking him back a little and surprising him a lot. "Every time we work on a case with Mary, she puts herself in danger," Rosie said. "She sacrifices for everyone else. She helps everyone else. And what do I do?"

"Rosie, you help," Mary said. "You always help."

"I make cookies," she argued, popping Stanley's chest with her finger again. "I cook, I bake. Oh, look out, Rosie, you might do something dangerous, like get burned on the stove. The rest of you protect me while you get involved."

"Rosie, darling, you do much more than that," Ian said.

She glared at him. "Don't try to sweet talk me, Ian," she said. "I know who I am and I know my limitations. But this time," she took a shuddering breath. "This time, the man involved saved my life. This time I'm the one who was saved. This time I had to do more."

Unheeded, tears flowed down her cheeks. "This time I wanted to make a difference."

Stanley put his arms around her and held her tightly. He placed a kiss on her head. "You make a difference every day," he whispered softly, "by just being you."

She sniffled. "But I needed to help Coach Thorne," she said. "Can you understand that?"

"Yeah, I can," he said, nodding his head. "I just ain't used to my sweet Rosie turning into a superhero."

Chuckling weakly, she stepped out of Stanley's arms, wiped her eyes and turned to the others. "Can you forgive me?"

Mary came up and put her arms around Rosie. "There is nothing to forgive," she said. "You followed your heart, that's always the best course of action."

"Aye, although it would be a terrible crime if you gave up cooking altogether," Ian said with a wink.

She giggled. "Oh, don't worry," she said. "I'll still bake."

Ian put his hand on his heart. "Well, saints be praised," he said. "We won't have to only eat Mary's cooking."

Mary whipped a couch pillow at him, hitting him in the stomach. "Eat that, MacDougal."

"Well, now that things are getting back to normal, we oughtta be putting together a plan to solve this case and keep my Rosie safe," Stanley said. "So, what's the first step?"

## Chapter Twenty-eight

"So this is how swinging singles live in Chicago," Bradley said, following Sean up another flight of narrow stairs to his apartment on the fifth floor carrying a bag of White Castle sliders.

"Yeah, great, ain't it?" Sean said with a grin, juggling his keys with the drink tray and the other bag, containing onion rings and French fries.

He pushed the door open and a huge orange cat nearly tripped him as he entered the apartment.

"Escapee from the zoo?" Bradley asked, watching the cat nearly topple Sean as it rubbed itself against his legs.

Sean grinned. "Bradley meet Tiny, Tiny meet Bradley."

Bradley followed Sean in and closed the door behind them. He looked anxiously around the room.

"What?" Sean asked.

"Well, if this is Tiny," Bradley joked, "I'm just concerned Monster is in the next room waiting to eat me for dinner."

Laughing, Sean placed the items in his hand on an already cluttered table, scooped Tiny up into his arms and gave him a vigorous head rubbing. "No, Tiny wasn't named because of his size," Sean said.

Bradley looked around and finally found a clear spot to place his things down. "Well, I wouldn't guess it was because of his appetite."

Sean shook his head. "No," he said. "Listen."

He lifted the cat up so they were face to face. "How's my big boy?" Sean asked.

Bradley could hear the cat's thunderous purring all the way across the room.

"How's my big boy?" Sean asked again.

The cat stopped purring for a moment, looked at Sean and opened its mouth. A tiny, barely audible "meow" was emitted.

Sean held the cat against his chest and rubbed him again, producing purrs that echoed through the apartment and probably the entire neighborhood. "See," Sean said. "Tiny is verbally challenged, all the other cats at the shelter used to pick on him, so I took him home with me."

"They wouldn't let poor Tiny join in any kitty-cat games?" Bradley asked with a grin.

Sean laughed. "Yeah, something like that. So, we keep each other company, share tuna sandwiches. It's all good."

He put Tiny down and walked across the room to a doorway. "I can loan you some sweats, if you don't mind CPD," he said.

"That's all Mary seems to wear around her place," Bradley said. "So they must be comfortable."

Sean came back in the room and tossed Bradley a sweat shirt and sweat pants. "Well, you can't keep them," he said. "But if you're nice to me, I'll get you a set as a wedding present."

The comment hit Bradley like a ton of bricks. "A wedding," he said slowly, his eyes loosing focus. His legs felt weak and he blindly sat down, nearly crushing Tiny in the process. "I'm getting married."

Shaking his head, Sean walked over to him. "Well, yeah, isn't that what happens when you ask someone to marry you?"

Still staring into space, Bradley nodded. "Yeah, I guess," he said. "But, you know, it was more…I love her…I want to be with her for the rest of my life."

"You forgot about all that complicated stuff in between, huh?"

Bradley nodded slowly. "I really hate weddings," he admitted.

Sean sat down on the edge of his coffee table, unbuttoned his uniform shirt and slipped it off. "Well, if you thought you hated weddings before, you ain't seen nothing yet," Sean said. "An Irish wedding is the wedding of all weddings."

Bradley dropped his head into his hands. "Think we could elope?"

"Hah, not if you want my mother to ever speak to you again," he said. "She's waited her whole life to plan Mary's wedding."

Bradley sighed. "Well, it's only one day."

"Oh, didn't you know," Sean said. "Irish weddings last a week."

Bradley's head shot up. "What?"

177

Sean laughed at him. "You should have seen your face. Priceless!"

"Not funny," he said, and then he noticed a large scar on Sean's arm. "Wow, that looks bad. Knife wound?"

Sean looked down at his arm. The scar had been there so long he barely thought of it. There were four slashes, evenly spaced and a puncture mark at the end of the one on the bottom. Even though they had healed years ago, they still had an ugly pink look to them.

"No, I got these when I visited Ireland when I was twelve," he said. "We were playing hide and seek near my grandmother's home and I went to hide in the woods. I must have encountered a pretty fierce thorn tree because I came out all bloodied and woozy. My brothers found me steps away from the woods and helped me back to the house."

"Wow," Bradley said. "Remind me to stay away from Irish woods."

Sean laughed. "Oh, the woods are nothing compared to Irish women."

They spent the evening watching basketball and complaining about the referees' eye-sight. It was nearly eleven when Sean grabbed a couple of blankets and a pillow and handed them to Bradley before he went to bed.

"I think I might have an extra toothbrush in the bathroom," he said, "in one of the drawers."

Bradley nodded. "Thanks, appreciate it."

Once Sean closed the door to his bedroom, Bradley sat down on the couch next to Tiny and pulled out his phone. He punched in Mary's number.

"Hello," a slightly drowsy voice responded.

"It sounds like I woke you up," he said. "I'm sorry. I'll call back tomorrow."

"Bradley?" her voice sounded more alert. "No, don't call back. I'm awake."

"You sure?"

"Yes, I'm sure," she said. "Are you home? Do you want to come over?"

He relaxed against the back of the couch and absently stroked Tiny. "I'm in Chicago," he said. "I'm at Sean's place."

"Well then you must have met Tiny," she said.

He could hear the laughter in her voice.

"As a matter of fact, I do believe that Tiny is sharing his bed with me tonight," he said.

She laughed. "Well, you won't be cold."

"I met Pete O'Bryan today."

"Really? Pete's a good guy. We've known him forever."

"He's going to help me find my daughter. And the guy is amazing."

"That's wonderful," she said. "I've never known Pete to lose a case."

"Yeah, he seems like the guy you want on your side," Bradley agreed. "I really feel hopeful about finding her."

"You should," Mary said. "You will."

He paused for a moment. "Mary, I can't begin to tell you how much meeting you has changed my life."

She laughed nervously. "Yeah, well, that whole seeing dead people can alter things a bit."

Chuckling, he shook his head. "No, I mean without you…there are so many things that happened today that are a direct result from meeting you."

"Bradley, Mike told us what you had to do today," she said. "I'm so sorry. How did things go?"

"Well, actually, much better than I thought," he admitted. "Bernie was great. He really knows what he's doing."

"Yeah, he's the best."

"I've got to ask, how many nephews does that guy have?"

Mary laughed. "There's got to be hundreds of them."

"Thank you."

"For what?"

"For letting me into your life and into your extended family," he said. "I know things moved faster and smoother because I was a friend of the O'Reilly clan."

"Well, that just part of the deal," she said softly.

"What deal?" he asked.

"When one O'Reilly loves you, the rest of them do too."

"Mary, that makes me slightly uncomfortable knowing Sean is sleeping in the next room."

She laughed again. "I didn't mean it that way."

"Mary."

"Yes Bradley."

"I love you."

She sighed. "I love you too."

"Good night. Sweet dreams."

"Yeah, you and Tiny too."

# Chapter Twenty-nine

Mary smiled and slowly sunk back into her bedding, she was just so much in love it almost scared her. She chuckled as she reviewed the conversation in her mind. She'd have to thank Sean for bringing Pete in on the case. She felt even more hopeful that Bradley was going to find his daughter.

She yawned and stretched her arms. It had been a busy day and tomorrow she was going to be even busier. Katie Brennan called after dinner and had a chance to speak with both Andy and Maggie. But after the phone call, there had been homework to do, baths to supervise, stories to read and arguments to mediate. She really didn't know how Katie did it every day and look so young and fresh. She was exhausted.

Closing her eyes, she quickly drifted into a deep sleep.

The room was getting colder and Mary automatically reached for her thick quilt, but could only find a thin cotton blanket. She pulled it up over her shoulders, but she was still cold. What had happened to her down quilt?

She opened her eyes and looked around. She was confused, the room was too dark. Did the streetlight outside burn out again?

She reached out toward her bed stand, but found her hand was tied with a thick rope. What the hell?

She sat up and realized she wasn't in her bed. Instead, she was on a couch in a cold, damp basement. She was *there* again. Looking down at her body, she saw her swollen abdomen and felt the child move inside of her. Reaching forward, she placed her hands against her stomach and felt a tiny kick vibrate against her hand.

A combination of awe and fear warred within her. This child, her child, was in danger. Instinctually defensive, she leaned forward, softly rubbing against the tiny foot lodged against her skin. "I'll protect you," she promised. "I'll keep you safe."

"I'm the one who will keep her safe," a deep voice taunted from the shadows of the room. "She's my daughter."

Scooting back as far as she could, Mary pulled her legs up and wrapped her arms around them, protecting the baby. "Get away from me."

Gary strolled out of the shadows, a blanket in his hands. "But, darling, if I leave who will keep you warm? Who will give you food?"

"I don't want anything from you," she whispered fiercely. "I want you to leave."

He slowly stroked her from the top of her head down along the side of her face, his hand lingering on her cheek. "But if I leave you, your baby will die," he said. "You don't want your baby to die, do you?"

She whimpered. "Please, please don't hurt my baby," she cried.

He sat next to her on the bed and smiled. "Oh course, I won't hurt her," he said. "As long as you do what I say."

He licked his lips and brushed her hair away from her face. "Will you do everything I say?"

She nodded, tears flowing down her face.

"Good girl," he mocked. "Now lie back on the couch so I can look at you."

She hesitated.

"You don't want your baby to die, do you?"

She unwrapped her arms and slowly leaned back against the couch.

"Excellent, excellent," he said eagerly. "Now, straighten your legs."

She lowered her legs to the couch and stared up at the pipes crisscrossing on the ceiling.

He lifted her shirt, exposed her belly and rubbed it slowly with both hands. "Oh, yes, our baby. Our creation," he murmured.

His touch made her skin crawl. She wanted to be sick. "Please don't touch me," she begged. "Please don't touch me."

"Oh, Mary, this is just the beginning of what I'm going to do to you," he said softly, sliding his hands to the waist of her pants. "And I'm going to enjoy every moment of it."

Panic filled her. She knew what he was going to do, had done before. "No," she screamed. "No, don't touch me."

Ian rushed into her room. "Mary, darling, listen to me," he said with a calm but forceful voice.

"Please, don't touch me," she cried.

"Darling, it's Ian," he said. "You have to fight him. You have to be stronger."

She tossed her head back and forth on her pillow. "He's going to hurt me again," she cried. "He's touching me…oh, no, please make him stop."

"Mary, you lift your leg and you kick him with all you've got," Ian commanded.

He saw her thrash her leg under the cover and kick out.

"Aye, that's my girl," he said. "Now kick him again. Harder."

He moved closer and sat next to her on the edge of the bed. "Now you're winning the fight," he said. "Are your hands loose, darling?"

"They're tied," she whimpered. "He's tied them with rope."

"Well, darling, you just need to pull them apart and you can break through that rope," he said. "Just pull at them, you'll see."

He watched her jerk her arms in her sleep. "They're off," she said, her breathing short and panicked. "They're off."

"Aye, now you can give him what for," he said. "You're in charge, Mary O'Reilly. Kick his ass."

The quick right cross seemed to come out of nowhere, but one moment Ian was sitting on the side of her bed and the next he was on the floor, nursing a bruised jaw. "Well, you probably took him down with that one," he said.

"Ian, is Mary going to die?" Maggie cried from the doorway. "Is someone trying to hurt her?"

Ian got up and hurried over to Maggie. He wrapped her in his arms for a moment. "Ach, no, she was just having a nightmare," he said. "That's all. And when our Mary has nightmares she gets a little loud."

Mike appeared next to her. "I'm sorry, I tried to comfort her, but she was worried about Mary."

"Ian," Mary sat up in her bed. "What's wrong?"

"Oh nothing," he said. "Nothing t'all."

"You was having a scary nightmare," Maggie said. "You was yelling really loud and I was scared."

Mary felt her heart drop; she slipped out of her bed and hurried over to Maggie. "Oh, sweetheart, I am so sorry I scared you," she said.

Maggie moved from Ian's arms into Mary's. "A bad man was trying to get you," she said. "I thought the bad man was in the house."

Biting her lower lip and blinking back her tears, Mary held the little girl close. "Oh, no, sweetheart, you're safe in this house," she said. "You have Ian and Mike and me to look after you. We won't let anyone hurt you."

"But the bad man was hurting you," she said. "I heard you screaming."

"Only in my dreams, sweetheart," Mary explained. "And then Ian came in and helped me. Sometimes big people need protectors too."

Maggie looked over at Ian. "He protects you too?" she asked. "Like Mike protects me?"

Mary nodded. "Yes, he does," she said. "He's very good at that."

Maggie yawned widely. "I'm going to marry him," she said with a sleepy voice.

"Well, that's a wise choice indeed," Mary said, cuddling the child for a few more moments. "Can I put you back in bed?"

"Mmmmm-hmmmm," Maggie mumbled.

Lifting her up in her arms, Mary carried her down the hall. Ian opened the door and drew down the blankets. Mike hovered nearby as Mary placed her into the bed and kissed her forehead. "Sweet dreams, sweetheart," she whispered to the little girl who was already asleep.

"I'll stay in here, just in case she wakes up," Mike whispered.

Mary nodded and she and Ian softly closed the door and walked down the hallway. Ian motioned for Mary to follow him downstairs and she led the way without saying a word.

He walked over to the stove and put the kettle on. Mary sat at the table and cradled her head in her hands. "I frightened her, Ian," she said. "I woke her from her sleep and frightened her."

He came over and sat next to her at the table. "You didn't mean to do it," he said. "And judging by how quickly she fell back to sleep, there were no residual effects."

"But what if I keep having them?" she asked, looking up at him. "What if I never get over...?"

He shook his head. "You've had less than a week to get over a traumatic situation. Why don't you give yourself a bit of a break?"

"But we don't know if I'll ever get over it," she said.

"Aye, but I believe as we change the circumstances in your dreams, so you're not the victim anymore, the dreams will lessen."

She closed her eyes for a moment. "I remember hearing your voice," she said, concentrating on the memory. "I remember you telling me to kick him."

"Aye, and you did."

She nodded. "I did. And I kicked him again and then I broke the ropes he tied on my wrists."

"And then you gave him a fine right cross," Ian said, rubbing his chin.

Her eyes widened. "Oh, Ian, did I hit you?" she asked.

"Me own fault," he said. "Here I am acting like your boxing coach and don't have enough sense to stand out of the way."

She allowed herself to smile. "I knocked him out cold," she said.

"That's me girl," he said. "You're a fighter, Mary O'Reilly, not a victim. You just have to try and remember that."

## Chapter Thirty

The bar was nearly empty. The owner was wiping down the tables and collecting the glasses. But in the far corner, two men sat together in the shadows nursing their glasses of beer.

"Okay, Wally, what's the big emergency?"

Wally sipped his beer, leaving a trail of froth on his upper lip. "Do you remember Rosie Meriwether?"

"Yeah, she's a real estate broker in town now," he replied. "Still looks pretty good and I hear she's widowed again."

"She came to see me," Wally interrupted, "wanted access to the high school."

"So?" he responded. "What's the big deal?"

"She's got this friend who's a parapsychologist."

"What the hell is that?"

"It's a ghost hunter," Wally said. "They use all this equipment to see if there are really ghosts in a place."

"Yeah, so, this is like reality TV, Wally."

"She wants to investigate the death of Coach Thorne," he said, lowering his voice.

A glass of beer dropped on the table and splashed over the rim. "What the hell?"

Wally nodded. "Yeah, she wants access to the chemistry lab so they can see if it's haunted."

Wally's companion took a deep breath and then sat back in his chair. "So what," he said. "I've seen those TV shows. All they do is report there's a ghost there. No big deal. They can't prove nothing."

Wally shook his head. "That isn't all," he said. "Rosie, she told me the reason this guy contacted her and wants to work with her…"

"Yeah, why?"

"Because she can talk to ghosts."

## Chapter Thirty-one

"Bradley, it's so good to see you," Maggie O'Reilly said, giving him a warm hug. "I'm so glad you could come for breakfast."

"Thank you for inviting me," he said. "It smells great in here."

She smiled. "Well, thank you," she said. "One of my Timmy's favorite meals is breakfast, so we try to have it together as often as we can."

"Morning, Ma," Sean said, dropping a kiss on her cheek and sweeping the petite woman up into a bear hug. "How's the new washer?"

She put her hands on her hips and tightened her lips. "It's fine," she said. "And if I see either you or your father sniffing around it, I'll bring my rolling pin to you."

Sean grinned. "Yes, ma'am."

"Um, is Mr. O'Reilly, I mean, Tim, around?" Bradley asked.

Maggie nodded. "Yes, he's in the living room with the twins," she said. "Why don't you join him in there while I finish making breakfast?"

"Come on, Bradley," Sean said. "I'll bring you in."

Bradley took a deep breath and nodded. "Thanks, I appreciate it."

They entered the living room to find Mary's father arguing with his sons, Arthur and Thomas. "Are you both daft?" he asked. "He was clearly fouled."

"Are you talking about that play in the second quarter?" Sean asked as they walked in the room.

Mary's father, Timothy, turned and looked at them. "Bradley, good to see you," he said warmly. "Yes, Sean, it was a clear foul."

Sean nodded. "I agree, but Bradley thought he was fine."

"What? You thought the call was good?" Timothy said, incredulously.

Bradley felt his stomach drop to his feet. "Well, from my point of view," Bradley said, with a gulp. "It looked good."

"See, Dad, we told you," Art said.

Bradley turned to Sean. "Thanks," he whispered. "Thanks a lot."

Sean grinned. "Hey, just trying to break the ice."

Timothy shook his head. "Next you'll tell me you thought the call in the third quarter was bad," he said.

"Well, as a matter of fact," Sean began. "Bradley thought…"

Bradley elbowed Sean. "Shut up, Sean," he whispered fiercely.

Sean chuckled. "Hey, Da, Bradley needs to talk to you," he said. "And you better do it now or he won't be able to enjoy breakfast."

Timothy stood up. "You need to speak with me?" he asked.

Bradley nodded. "Yes sir, I do."

"Come on," he said. "Let's go out to the back yard. We can have a little privacy there."

They walked out through a patio door and down a path that led to a large garden. "I like puttering around in here during the spring and summer," Timothy said. "When things grow, it's like a little miracle. You get this small seed, you stick it in the dirt, water it and then you get a tomato plant."

"I used to have a garden," Bradley said. "When I lived in Sycamore."

"Sean told us about your wife and your daughter," Timothy said. "I want you to know how sorry I am for you, for your loss."

"Thank you," Bradley said. "I couldn't have ever discovered what had happened to her without Mary. And Sean has been so helpful. I owe your family a great deal."

Timothy nodded and walked forward. "So, you came to my house to thank me?" he asked.

Bradley shook his head. "No. I mean I am grateful, but that's not why I'm here," he said. "I...I love Mary."

"Yeah, well, that's understandable," Timothy said. "She's a lovely person."

"No, I mean, I love her," he said. "And I want to ask her to marry me."

Timothy scratched his head. "So, you just discover what happened to your wife and now you want to marry my daughter. Don't you think it's pretty fast?"

"I think I've been in love with Mary since the moment I met her," he explained. "But I couldn't act on it because I didn't know what happened to Jeannine. I searched for her for eight years, without ever being unfaithful. Mary is the only woman who makes me feel this way."

Timothy nodded and rubbed his chin with his hand. "You've got a daughter?"

Bradley nodded.

"And even without knowing her," Timothy said. "You'd give your life for her, you'd die for her."

Once again, Bradley nodded.

"So, Mary's my little girl," he said, looking up and meeting Bradley's eyes. "And you're asking me to let you have her. How do I know you're good enough? How do I know you're going to take care of her?"

Bradley ran his hand through his hair. "Well, I'm not good enough for her," he said. "She's amazing. She loves unconditionally, she gives without question. She is braver, stronger and nobler than I will ever be. But for some reason, she loves me. What I can promise you is she will never want for anything. She will never doubt my love. Nothing will ever be more important in my life than Mary."

Timothy nodded slowly. "And what happens if I say no?"

Closing his eyes, Bradley felt his heart shatter within his chest. He took a deep breath and faced Timothy. "If you say no, then I won't ask her to marry me," he said. "Her family, all of you, mean too much to her for me to cause a rift in it."

"You wouldn't ask her anyway and let her choose what she wants?"

He shook his head. "No, because either choice would hurt her. I never want to hurt her."

Timothy turned away from Bradley and stared at a playground set in the far corner of the yard for a few moments. "I built that playground set for Mary," he said. "She'd spend hours on it. Never swinging on it, like normal kids. No, she'd climb all over it."

Bradley couldn't think of anything to say. Was Timothy changing the subject? Was the conversation over? Was he finally going to be able to marry her, only to be turned away by her father?

Timothy took a deep breath. "Are you going to find your daughter?" he asked.

"Yes, I am, I will find my daughter."

Timothy turned back and nodded his head. "Good. Good. I need a granddaughter to play on that playground."

Bradley inhaled deeply. "You mean...?" he asked.

Timothy patted him on the shoulder. "Welcome to the family, Bradley," he said, with a smile. "Take care of my little girl."

# Chapter Thirty-two

Mary walked down the stairs slowly, still tired from the night before.

"Shhhh, don't tell her," she heard Maggie say. "It's a s'prize."

"Aye, darling, we'll just keep it our little secret," Ian said.

"She's gonna like it all right," Andy offered. "She likes stuff like that."

Mary felt her heart melt and warmth replace the fatigue from the night before. How was she ever going to be able to let those two go home? She rubbed her hand over her heart.

"She's coming," Maggie said. "I can hear her."

Mary hurried down the remainder of the stairs and walked into the kitchen. "Good morning," she said brightly.

Maggie and Andy stood up, their hands behind their backs. "We made something for you," Maggie announced. "Something you're gonna love."

"What is it?" she asked.

"Breakfast!" Andy said.

They brought their hands forward. Maggie was holding a large glass of chocolate milk, with extra syrup running down the sides. "I made it myself," she said. "It has lots of chocolate."

"LOTS of chocolate," Ian emphasized, from the other side of the counter.

Andy held out a peanut butter and jelly sandwich cut in diamonds. "I made this myself," he added proudly. "It's got peanut butter and jelly and raisins and marshmallows."

"Well, everything looks delicious," Mary said.

"And we colored on the plate," Maggie added. "See."

The paper plate had little hearts and squiggles drawn all over it. "It's the most beautiful plate I've ever seen."

"We already ate our breakfast, so we can watch you eat yours," Andy said.

Mary took a sip of the chocolate milk and realized Ian had not been joking. It tasted like the drink was half syrup and half milk. "This is the most chocolaty milk I've ever had," she said. "It's delicious."

She lifted a portion of the sandwich and took a big bite. "Mmmmm, good," she murmured, the roof of her mouth covered with peanut butter. "Delicious."

"See, there, I told you she'd love it," Ian said, carrying a cup of tea to her.

"To help you wash things down," he whispered.

Then she saw Ian's face, covered with a bruise the size of an orange.

She placed her hand over her mouth in dismay. "Oh, Ian, I'm so sorry," she said. "That looks awful."

"Ian told us he got it when he was fighting a monster last night," Andy said. "A huge monster. Twenty feet tall."

Mary grinned. "Twenty feet tall?" she gasped. "Oh, my, where did you find such a beast?"

Ian looked slightly discomfited. "Aye, well, it was in the wee hours of the morning," he said. "And I was...I was stepping outside because I heard a noise."

"Don't you know you're not supposed to go outside when you hear noises?" Andy lectured. "That's what always gets the guys killed in the movies."

"He's right, Ian," Mary agreed, walking toward the counter and picking up an extra piece of toast slathered with marmalade. "And movies never lie."

"Unlike some Scottish professors I know," she whispered.

Ian coughed. "Well, and I was afraid it was going to come into the house," he said. "So I was willing to take the risk."

Maggie giggled. "Mike would have saved us," she said.

"Mike is another one of her imaginary friends," Andy explained. "She even talks to him at night."

Maggie turned and grinned at Mike who was standing in the corner. He winked at her and then stuck out his tongue at Andy, which made the little girl giggle even more.

Andy shook his head. "Sometimes things are weird at your house, Mary."

Mary laughed out loud. "Oh, Andy, I totally agree with you."

"I told Mom about Mike yesterday when she called," Maggie said. "She said he was probably a guardian angel."

"Moms have to say stuff like that so they don't hurt your feelings," Andy responded.

Ian chuckled. "I'm sure you have at least two guardian angels looking out for you," he said to Andy.

Grinning, Andy nodded. "Yeah, Mom says my guardian angel must be exhausted by the end of the day."

"Aye, like Mary's guardian angels," Ian said, winking at her.

"Mary has more than one?" Andy asked.

"Oh, aye, she needs a whole army of them."

"Okay, it's time to brush your teeth and get ready for the bus," Mary interrupted. "We don't want you to be late for school."

Maggie sighed. "You sounded just like a mom when you said that."

"Thank you, Maggie," Mary said with a sad smile.

A few minutes later, Mary opened the door to let the children out and found Rosie and Stanley ready to knock. "Well, good morning," Mary said, as Andy and Maggie brushed past her.

"Good morning," Rosie said. "I baked some cookies for some good children to have when they get home from school. Do you know any good children?"

"I'm good," Maggie said. "I'm very good."

"Me too," Andy agreed, he paused for a moment and added. "Most of the time."

"Well, I think most of the time is good enough for chocolate chip cookies," Rosie said. "Don't you think?"

Andy nodded eagerly. "Yeah, I do."

"Well, then, hurry off to school, so you can hurry home," she said.

The children ran down the steps to the waiting bus.

"You'd better hide those cookies from Ian or there won't be any left for the kids," Mary warned with a smile, inviting them into the house.

"I heard that, Mary O'Reilly," Ian called, walking in from the kitchen.

"What the hell happened to you?" Stanley exclaimed.

"I went a round with a famous Irish pugilist," he said. "And I lost."

"Mary did that to you?" Stanley replied, his eyes narrowing as he approached Ian. "What did you do to her?"

Mary stepped between them. "I was having a nightmare, a flashback, and Ian was helping me," she said. "In my dream I was punching Gary, unfortunately…"

"You got quite an arm Mary," Stanley said, examining the bruise.

"To say nothing of the fist attached to it," Ian added.

"Well, if it makes you feel any better, I have some cookies just for you," Rosie said, laying a plate of cookies on the coffee table. "I remembered how much you enjoyed these the last time I made them.

Ian picked up a cookie and took a bite. "I'm feeling better already," he sighed, savoring the taste of the cookie.

Mary reached for one and Ian snatched the plate away from her. "I'm sorry, young lady," he said. "You can't have any cookies until you've finished your breakfast."

"You want a bruise on the other side?" she asked.

He handed over a cookie. "You've a way with words, Mary," he said.

Rosie sat down on the couch and cleared her throat. "We do need to get ready," she said. "Stevo Morris will be here any moment."

"Who's Stevo Morris?" Ian asked.

"He was the shortstop on the high school baseball team," Rosie explained. "The one who helped the coach get all of the students out of the room."

201

"He was the last person to see Coach Thorne alive?" Mary asked.

Rosie nodded. "The coach helped him down and he was waiting for the coach to come next. He hit the ground, turned around to help the coach and the explosion knocked him to the ground."

"That's pretty traumatic," Ian said.

"Yeah, he blamed himself for a long time," Rosie said. "If he'd been faster the coach would have made it out safely."

"Well, it will be interesting to interview him." Mary said. "When is he supposed to arrive?"

A knock on the door delayed any answer.

Mary walked over to the door and opened it. On the other side was a tall, thin man with a badly scarred face, bright blue eyes and a thick shock of white hair. "Mary O'Reilly?" he asked politely.

Mary smiled. "Yes, hi, you must be Mr. Morris."

"Stevo," he said, with a shy smile, "and this is my wife, Lo."

He stepped to the side and Mary saw the tall blonde woman standing next to him. Although Mary guessed she was also in her sixties, she was the kind of woman whose bone structure and perfect skin made her ageless. Her hair was cut in a fashionable bob and she was dressed in jeans and a fitted sweater.

"Hello," Lo said, her voice soft and timid. "I hope you don't mind that I tagged along."

"No, I don't mind at all," Mary said, with a welcoming smile. "The more information we can get, the better. Please come in."

Rosie performed introductions and the group sat around the fireplace in the living room.

"Do you remember how the fire started?" Mary asked.

"It started at my lab table," he said. "We were adding distilled water to ammonium nitrate, I'll never forget that."

"That shouldn't have caused an explosion," Ian said.

"No, it shouldn't have," Stevo agreed. "And there were other students whose experiments did what they were supposed to do. But the stuff in my beaker started foaming up and getting hot. The coach yelled at me to step back."

"So, you're sure the other experiments worked," Mary said.

"Yeah, I remember Jon saying it was freezing."

"Can we speak with Jon?" Ian asked.

Stevo shook his head. "No, Jon died in Vietnam," he explained. "But when the investigator from B&R interviewed us, Jon said his experiment was fine. If they still have a record of the fire, that interview ought to be in it."

"Why did the investigator interview the students?" Mary asked.

Stevo shook his head. "Someone was trying to call it negligence and they wanted to blame the coach. There was a pretty big deal made of it."

"I didn't know that," Rosie said.

"Yeah, well, it was mostly the guys on the baseball team who were interviewed," he said. "All the guys knew the coach was a stand-up guy. No way was he careless."

"The coach was a hero," Lo added fervently. "He looked out for all of the students, not just on the team or in his classes."

She paused for a moment and then reached over and clasped her husband's hand. He met her eyes and nodded, patting her hand.

"He saved a lot of lives," she said. "He was one of the good guys. He didn't care if you were rich and powerful or just one of the little people. He stood up for what was right."

"Tell me what happened before the explosion," Mary prompted.

"Me and the coach got everyone else out of the room," he said. "Then the coach told me it was my turn. He told me he'd jump down after me and wanted me to catch him. So, he lowered me down as far as he could and then I dropped and rolled."

Stevo shook his head.

"It wasn't more than a minute later, I stood up to catch him and the whole place exploded. It was like the Fourth of July."

"Why do you say that?"

"Because there were sparks, like fireworks, coming out of the window."

"Where was the coach standing when he dropped you out the window?" Mary asked.

"We were at the window at the front of the class because the smoke from the back of the room was moving up," he said. "He was facing the window, because he was letting me down."

"Was there a fire in the front of the room?" she asked, remembering the burns on the right side of the coach's face.

He shook his head. "No, it was all in the back, but it was slowly moving forward," he said.

"Is there any reason the coach would have turned away from the window, gone back into the room?"

"No, everyone was out. All he had to do was climb onto the windowsill," he said. "But the explosion happened too fast. It didn't give him a chance."

"Do you remember anything odd about the explosion?" she asked. "Do you remember what it smelled like?"

Stevo's eyes widened and he shook his head. "Yeah, now that you mention it, I do remember that it smelled like garlic bread. It was so weird."

Mary wrote down the word "Phosphorus" and then looked back at Stevo and Lo. "Was there anyone who would have wanted to kill the coach?"

Stevo shook his head. "No. No, everyone loved Coach Thorne."

Lo looked up and then lowered her head, not meeting Mary's eyes. "No," she said. "No."

Mary put her notepad down. "Well, thank you," she said. "You've been very helpful."

"If there's anything else we can do," Stevo said. "Just let us know."

Mary nodded. "Thanks, I might just do that."

# Chapter Thirty-three

"Are you sure you don't want me to come in with you?" Mary asked Ian.

They were sitting in the parking lot of B&R Manufacturing on the outskirts of Freeport.

"Aye, let me go in first," he said. "Then if we have some follow up questions, you can go in without raising suspicions. Besides, I'm a college professor; I'm used to dealing with stuffy administrators."

He hopped out of the Roadster and entered the front door. The wooden-paneled lobby and tile floor spoke of the years of success in the farming community. The large portraits of the former presidents spoke of the obvious pride they had in their business.

Ian tugged at the sleeves of his suit coat and made sure he was in pristine condition before he approached the front desk. "Hello," the burly man at the front desk said. "Can I help you."

*Half receptionist, half security guard*, Ian thought. *I wonder why they feel the need for both?*

"Good afternoon, I'm Professor Ian MacDougal," Ian began.

"If you're looking for a grant you have to request a form through our website," the man interrupted.

"Well, thank you, but I'm not interested in a grant," Ian said. "I'm here…"

"If you're looking for a job in our research department, we are currently not seeking new employees, but feel free to fill out an employment form on our website."

"Again, thank you, but I'm not searching for employment, either," Ian said, curtly. "I'd like to speak…"

"If you need information about our products for your research, please see our specific product pages on…"

"I know, your website," Ian interrupted. "I'm working with the Chicago Police Department. And we can make this hard or we can make this easy."

The man sat up in his chair and shook his head. "What?"

*Well, damn, those stupid movie lines really do work*, Ian thought.

"I'm working with the Chicago Police Department and the University of Chicago," he said. "I'm working on case that requires me to speak with the president of your company. I called earlier to see if he was available and I was told to come here. I could get a warrant if you'd like, but then I'd be obliged to make anything I find public record. Your choice."

"Um, let me call Mr. Brandlocker."

"I'd be much obliged," Ian said.

"Pardon?" the man asked, looking confused.

Ian sighed. "Thank you."

208

"Oh, hey, no problem."

A few minutes later Ian was ushered into the inner offices of B&R Manufacturing. A pert secretary offered him his choice of beverage and reading material and he assumed that he would be cooling his heels for quite a long time. However, he was pleasantly surprised to see the large oak door at the far end of the room open and an athletically built older man walk out.

"Professor MacDougal?" the man asked.

Ian stood and nodded. "Aye, that would be me."

"I'm Ephraim Brandlocker," the man said. "Please come into my office."

The office would have been considered luxurious on Michigan Avenue, in Freeport it seemed so out of place it was almost decadent.

Ephraim slid onto his leather chair and brushed his hand over the polished mahogany and ivory inlaid desk. "I like nice things," he said.

"It seems you do," Ian said, noting both the desk and many of the art objects on the shelves and walls were obviously smuggled into the United States because they were considered contraband. "And it's obvious you like a little…risk…in your decorating choices."

Laughing, Ephraim opened a drawer and pulled out a Cuban cigar which he offered to Ian. "The best isn't always the…easiest to obtain," he said. "But I always get what I want."

Ian smiled and shook his head, turning down the cigar. "Ach, no, it'd be a shame to get used to the taste of those on a college professor's salary," he said.

"Ah, yes, a college professor," Ephraim repeated. "I took a few minutes to check your references. The Chicago Police Department speaks highly of your skills."

Ian nodded, acknowledging his remark.

"And you're no ordinary college professor," he said, "with a professor's salary. You and I have a lot in common."

"Do we?" Ian asked.

"We both have a lineage that not only sets us above the others around us, but requires more from us than the average citizen," he said. "I believe in the UK you call it *noblesse oblige*."

"Actually, that would be French," Ian said. "But we borrow their words all the time. It makes us sound much more sophisticated than we actually are. You'd know about that, wouldn't you, Ephraim?"

Ephraim's eyes narrowed. "You came here wanting something from me, I believe," he said. "And you choose to be rude. Maybe you don't know who you're dealing with."

"Oh, perhaps you didn't know this about the Scots," Ian said, standing and leaning over the table. "Let me enlighten you. We are a warrior people. We're often crass. We don't do things in a small way. Hell, we flip telephone poles across a field as a national sport. We wear kilts, because, quite frankly, no one dare stop us. And we don't put up with a lot of crap. You're wasting my time, Mr. Brandlocker. I've already mentioned to my friends in Chicago I might need a warrant to search your files. It'll take a day to get here. And with it will also come several other investigators looking through your files. But I'd rather wait a day than sit here listen to you tell me how great you are for another minute."

Ian turned to leave.

"Wait," Ephraim called out. "What do you want?"

"The fire investigation file for the chemistry lab explosion in the 1960s," he said.

Ephraim reached across his desk, picked up a manila envelope and handed it to Ian.

"I know what's going on in my town, Professor. I have a feeling that we might have both underestimated each other," Ephraim said.

Ian shook his head. "No, I understand you completely."

# Chapter Thirty-four

"Mr. Gormley will be happy to see you now," the assistant said, ushering Rosie back into Walter's office.

Walter stood and extended his hand. "Thank you for coming back to see me," he said.

"Well, I did promise you that I would give you updates," she said. "There isn't much news. But we do feel that it was more than an accident. Perhaps there was a secondary explosion and that's what killed Coach Thorne. But tonight is the first night we're going to use the key. We going to go over late tonight and try to get in touch with his spirit."

"Tonight?" he repeated. "You're going to go tonight?"

Rosie nodded. "Yes, um, the atmosphere is, um, primed for psychic phenomena. So, we should be able to speak with him."

"I find this highly interesting, Rosie," Walter said. "There is so much in the world we don't know about."

"Indeed," Rosie replied.

"And you see ghosts?" he repeated.

"Yes, yes I do."

"And Professor MacDougal, remind me again, does he see ghosts?"

Rosie shook her head, concentrating on getting the answers right. "Oh, no, he just has equipment to record them."

"Special equipment?"

"Yes, very special equipment," she said, praying he didn't ask her to name them.

"And where is Professor MacDougal staying?"

"Oh, at Mary's house," Rosie said, relieved to know the answer.

She clapped her hands over her mouth. "Oh, dear, I wasn't supposed to mention that."

"Well, Rosie, you and I are old friends," he said. "Don't worry; your secret is safe with me. So, that would be Mary…"

"O'Reilly, Mary O'Reilly," Rosie said. "But she can't see ghosts at all. She has never been able to see ghosts."

Rosie giggled. "It would be totally absurd to think that Mary O'Reilly could see ghosts."

Walter nodded his head. "Well, I'm sure seeing a ghost is a very rare ability, Rosie. And certainly not everyone can do it. So, I don't think less of your friend if she can't see ghosts."

Rosie took a deep breath and smiled. "Thank you, Walter; that was the perfect thing to say."

# Chapter Thirty-five

The clock on the dashboard displayed 11:45 as they pulled into the teachers' parking lot at the high school. "Is there any reason we had to wait until nearly midnight to do this?" Ian asked.

"Midnight is so much better," Mary teased. "I wanted to be sure all the ghosts in the school were active."

"Oh, you're funny aren't you," he said.

"I thought you researched ghosts in Edinburgh Castle," she said. "You seem a bit jumpy for someone who's done this before."

"Scottish ghosts are much more reserved than your American ones," he said. "Our ghosts merely parade down a hall or appear near a battlement. There's no gadding about talking to people. It's much more dignified and stoic."

"Boring if you ask me," Mary said, grabbing her backpack and slipping it over her shoulder.

"There's not a thing wrong with boring," Ian said, grabbing his own backpack and following her across the darkened parking lot toward the entrance to the school.

They were nearly to the door when a dark figure stepped out from behind a tree. Ian jumped and Mary reached for a revolver she no longer carried.

"Going somewhere?" Bradley asked.

Mary grinned and jogged the last few yards. "You're back," she said, throwing her arms around his neck and kissing him soundly. "Welcome home."

"Well, you won't be getting that kind of a greeting from me," Ian said. "But it's good to have you back."

His arm still around Mary's waist, he chuckled. "A handshake would suffice."

"So how did you know we'd be here?" Mary asked.

"I called your house and Stanley told me where you were heading," he said, looking down at her. "I thought we decided you would be investigating something safe."

Mary shrugged her shoulders. "Bradley, this case is over forty years old and it's about an explosion in a chemistry lab," she said. "What could be safer?"

"And what you're not telling me is?"

She sighed. "He was probably murdered."

"Probably?" Bradley asked.

"Well, I still have to interview Coach Thorne," she said. "We didn't have enough time the other night…"

"When you were breaking and entering?" Bradley interrupted.

"Well, actually, we were merely entering," Ian said. "There was absolutely no breaking involved."

"But now we're legal," Mary added. "The superintendent gave us a key."

"Walter Formley?" Bradley asked. "He knows you're doing this?"

"Well, actually, he thinks Rosie is doing this," Mary said. "But he knows we're looking into the explosion."

"Okay, let's go in," Bradley said.

The halls were dark except for the small circles of illumination from the emergency lights every twenty feet. They made their way silently past the offices until they reached the stairwell. Their footsteps echoed as they climbed to the second floor.

"I love old schools," Mary whispered. "There are so many possibilities for ghosts."

"Really?" Bradley asked, following directly behind her. "What kind of possibilities?"

"In most schools there are former teachers who float down the halls retracing their steps in life," she said. "Then the librarians who still linger in the stacks, looking for students who aren't whispering. And then, the fiercest of all..."

"And who would those be?" Ian asked.

"The lunch ladies who float through the lunchroom, metal spoon still in hand."

A clatter at the end of the hall caused them all to stop in their tracks. "Okay, that wasn't a spirit," Bradley whispered. "So, for this one, I go first."

He quietly moved in front of Mary and took the remaining stairs two at a time, pausing at the entrance to the second floor hall. Mary came up behind him. "Are you armed?" he asked.

She shook her head.

"Then stay back," he ordered, pulling his service revolver out of his holster.

His back against the wall, he slipped into the hallway and, staying in the shadows, moved slowly toward the end of the hall. Mary waited a moment and started to move after him when Ian caught her arm. "He told you to stay," Ian whispered.

"He doesn't have backup," she said. "I have to go."

Ian rolled his eyes. "Fine, but I'm going as well."

They both slipped into the hall and followed Bradley, staying several yards behind him. Mary could see Bradley's shadow against the lockers when he approached the emergency light. He was moving forward, his gun pointing toward the floor. But then she saw a figure step out of the doorway behind him and pull a gun out.

"Bradley," she screamed. "Behind you."

Bradley turned and dropped. A gun fired and the emergency light exploded, plunging that portion of the corridor into darkness. Ian grabbed Mary and pulled her to the floor, just before a second bullet slammed into the lockers above them.

They heard running footsteps echo in the hall.

"Are you…?" Bradley called.

"I'm fine," she interrupted. "I'll call for back-up."

Bradley jumped up and ran in the direction of the gunman. He paused at the end of the corridor and listened. He heard a door close softly and muffled footsteps. Quickly moving forward, he found the second floor entrance to the auditorium. Dropping low, he opened the door and slipped inside. Once the door closed, the auditorium was pitch black inside. Bradley knew a flashlight would make him an easy target, so he stayed low and listened for movement.

He could hear a faint pattering of footsteps near the stage. "Police," he yelled, moving down the aisle toward the stage. "Freeze."

A brief sliver of light flooded the room as the door from the hallway on the other side of the auditorium was opened and a dark figure slipped through. Bradley ran down the aisle, guided by the soft chair lights on the end of the rows, and across the front of the room. He pushed open the door in time to hear the sound of an outside door slamming shut. He ran down the hallway, but there were a half dozen outside entrances on this side of the building and there was no way of telling which one the gunman had used.

"Damn," he swore, placing his gun back in its holster.

He pulled out his radio and called into dispatch. "Gunman escaped through one of the doors on the southeast side of the high school. All units should be on the lookout for a single figure, dressed in dark clothing in the area of the student parking lot, tennis courts, soccer field or baseball field. Be aware the suspect is armed and dangerous."

# Chapter Thirty-six

Mary and Ian stood outside, next to her car, as the police did a thorough search of the high school. "You know," Ian said. "I was just thinking if it had just been Rosie instead of you and Bradley, there might be two very dead ghost hunters."

Mary nodded. "I was thinking the same thing."

"So, this was much more than a mere accident in a chemistry lab," Ian said. "I think the man was murdered."

"And the murderer is still alive," Mary added.

Bradley walked across the lawn toward them, speaking with one of his officers. "Yes, I just want to take a few minutes with Miss O'Reilly and Professor MacDougal up on the second floor to see if they can recall anything about the suspect," he said. "I'd appreciate if you would watch the perimeter to ensure no one tries to get back in."

He looked up and met Mary's eyes, concern evident.

"Obviously the good police chief has come to the same conclusion we have," Ian said.

They walked over to Bradley, maintaining the appearance of being just witnesses to the crime. Mary took a deep breath. "Did you want to question us, Chief?" she asked.

"I'd like you to come back into the school with me," he said. "If we can retrace our steps, perhaps you can remember something important."

"Aye, we'd be happy to help you," Ian said.

They walked back to the front entrance and into the building. All the lights in the school were lit and the inside was now like midday. Bradley waited until they were in the stairwell, away from any doors and windows to stop and pull Mary into his arms. "I thought this was supposed to be a safe case," he said, holding her close for a moment. "When I heard that second shot…"

"Aye, that one was too close for comfort," Ian agreed. "And had you not been here tonight, Mary and I would have walked into an ambush."

Bradley released Mary and turned to Ian. "An ambush set for you and Rosie."

They started up the stairs once again. "I doubt it was a coincidence the gunman was here on the very day Rosie received the key," Ian said. "And now we have to solve the murder because we're the prime targets."

"Well, I guess the best place to start is the scene of the crime," Mary said, entering the chemistry lab.

The back of the room was still hidden in the shadows, but this time the lab tables were scattered with equipment for some kind of experiment the students would be performing the next day. The white board was covered with notes and a formula. Mary was happy to see the shades were still drawn;

she really didn't need anyone looking in on this conversation.

"Why isn't the door locked?" Bradley asked, following them into the room.

Mary came over and took Bradley's hand. He looked around the room and immediately spied the man in the shadows.

"Because I won't have another student locked in a burning room with no way to escape," the ghost said.

Bradley nodded, his heart beating a little faster. Would he ever get used to actually seeing ghosts? "Well, that sounds like a reasonable answer," he said. "You must be Coach Thorne."

"I go nearly fifty years without anyone being able to see me and in two days three people are talking to me," he said, moving out of the shadows. "What is this? A convention?"

Mary chuckled. "No, but it is somewhat out of the ordinary," she conceded. "This is Freeport's Poloce chief, Bradley Alden."

Charlie nodded his head in Bradley's direction. "Nice to meet you, Chief," he said.

"Bradley, please," he said. "I understand you're quite a hero. One of the people you saved is a dear friend of ours. We owe you a great deal."

"Rosie Meriwether," Charlie said with a smile. "Is she still an interesting combination of happiness, enthusiasm, love and eccentricity?"

They all laughed. "Aye, we call it *joie de vivre*," Ian said.

"Joy of life," Charlie said, nodding. "Yes, that describes her perfectly."

"Unfortunately, someone was trying to put an end to that life this evening," Bradley said. "There was a gunman waiting in the hall for her."

"A gunman," Charlie exclaimed. "For Rosie? Why?"

"Because they know she is investigating your death," Mary explained.

"Well, then, stop," Charlie said firmly. "I died to save people, not to have them killed."

Ian shook his head and rubbed the back of his neck. "Aye, and there's the rub," he said. "You thought you died saving people, but you were murdered."

"Murdered?" he replied. "No! I couldn't have. How?"

"That's what we'd really like to figure out," Mary said. "And now that Rosie's in danger, there's no going back."

Charlie paced across the room. "But I wasn't murdered," he insisted. "It was an experiment gone wrong. Faulty chemicals. Maybe a prank that got out of control. But murdered?"

He shook his head. "Why would someone want to murder me?"

"Charlie, I need you to think back to that day," Mary said. "Think back to when you were dropping Stevo out the window."

"Yeah, I remember it," he said. "Stevo was amazing. He kept his head and saved lives. There was no way I could have gotten all those kids out before the explosion."

"So, all the kids were out," Mary said. "It was just you and Stevo. Where was the fire?"

He walked up to the front window and faced the back of the room. "We were here," he said. "The smoke was getting pretty thick, we were coughing, but we could still see out the windows. I told Stevo I'd let him down and then I'd come down next."

He chuckled. "I made him promise not to whip me over to Smith for a double play."

"So, Stevo's safe," Mary said, she and Bradley walking over and joining Charlie at the window. "You're ready to climb out the window...then what happened?"

"Boom," Charlie said. "That's it, boom! Then it was over."

"Did you turn away from the window? Did you hear something? Did you hesitate?"

"Hell no," he said. "I wanted out. My foot was on the windowsill."

"Do remember the impact? Do you remember which way you were blown?"

He paused and thought about it for a moment. His face registered the shock of the dawning realization. "From the right," he said slowly, "the explosion came from the front of the class, not the back."

Mary nodded. "The explosion had nothing to do with the fire. Someone set a secondary explosion and detonated it once you were the only one left in the room."

## Chapter Thirty-seven

Charlie hovered over a lab stool next to one of the tables, his head resting in his scarred hands. "How could this…?" he stammered, his voice filled with bewilderment. "Why would someone…?"

"It never makes sense," Mary said.

He lifted his head, a different kind of pain etched in his eye. "But I thought the kids liked me."

"They loved you," she insisted. "The students we've spoken with loved you. You made a difference in their lives and they never forgot you."

"This didn't have to be the action of a student," Bradley added. "The security wasn't as tight in those days as it is today. Almost anyone could have gotten into the school and planted the bomb. Anyone with that kind of knowledge."

Charlie nodded his head. "I'm sorry, I know it's not helpful, but I can't think of anyone who wanted me dead."

"That's good," Ian inserted. "At least when we find the bugger it won't be a long list."

Charlie laughed bitterly. "Well, I hope not."

"So, let's first talk about the teachers you worked with," Mary suggested. "Were you up for tenure? Was there any competition?"

Charlie shrugged. "Yeah, as a matter of fact, I was up for department head," he said. "So was Ross Gormley, but he'd never do something like this."

"Gormley?" Bradley asked. "Was his son Walter Gormley?"

"Yeah, little Wally Gormley," Charlie acknowledged. "He was my student because a parent couldn't teach their own child. Not that much teaching got through Wally's head. He wasn't the sharpest tack in the box. What ever happened to him?"

Ian shook his head. "He's the superintendent of schools," he admitted.

"No, kidding," Charlie said. "Wow. I would have never guessed that one."

"But Wally was also the only other person who knew Rosie was coming up here tonight," Bradley said. "And it's obvious Ross Gormley would know how to create a bomb."

"And have access to your class," Mary added.

Charlie shook his head. "I can't see it," he said. "Ross was a good guy. He was my friend."

"Well, I recently learned you can't always rule out the guys you believe are your friends," Bradley said bitterly. "I suggest we put him on our list."

Charlie glided across the room and stood next to the front window. "Fine, you're the expert," he said. "What else do you need to know?"

"There was an inquiry after your death," Mary said. "Someone wanted you labeled as negligent. Did you hear anything about that?"

Charlie shook his head. "No," he said. "Really? After I saved those kids, someone wanted to blame me? My poor Betty. That must have been hell for her."

"Betty?" Bradley asked.

"My wife," he replied. "I left a wife and a little girl."

"Dr. Thorne is his daughter," Mary told Bradley.

"Well, then, I owe you a debt of gratitude," Bradley said. "Your daughter saved my life."

Charlie smiled. "She was always a bright little tyke," he said proudly. "I'm glad my death didn't hold her back."

He sighed sadly. "What else haven't I told you?"

"Were there any students who held a grudge against you?" Mary asked.

He shook his head. "No, this was a good year," he said. "The kids were great and the parents were fairly normal too."

"While you're thinking about that one, I have another question for you," Ian said. "Why would the folks at B&R Manufacturing be so interested in covering up what happened in here?"

"B&R Manufacturing?" Charlie asked. "Caleb Brandlocker?"

"Aye, well, now it's his son, Ephraim," he said.

Shaking his head, he glided back to stand in front of them. "You learn a lot about people when you coach their children," he said. "Some have illusions of grandeur for both themselves and their kids. I always feel sorry for the kids whose parents think high school baseball is a ticket to the major league. I mean, give the kid a break, this is Freeport and this is high school baseball."

Mary nodded. "I coached pee-wee baseball in Chicago," she said. "I had to throw parents out of the games more often than any of the kids. But I didn't have an issue from them because I carried a gun."

Charlie laughed. "Yeah, I should have been a cop," he agreed. "Those parents don't do their kids any good by making them think they are better than anyone else. They grow up to be delinquents."

"Ephraim Brandlocker?" Ian asked.

"He was gone, graduated by the time this happened," Charlie said. "He had a lot of issues, but it's not my story to tell. Sorry, that's all I can say."

"Anyone else?" Mary asked. "Anyone like Ephraim?"

Charlie shook his head. "No, like I said, this was a good year," he said. "I had a bunch of good players who knew what it was like to play as a team."

"You took State that year," Mary said.

"What?" Charlie asked.

"Stevo Morris told us the team took State that year," Mary said. "The boys wanted to do it for you. They didn't want you to be forgotten."

"For me?" Charlie asked, tears streaming down his cheek. "That...that means a lot. Thank you."

And then he faded away.

## Chapter Thirty-eight

Mary pulled her Roadster into the driveway and watched through the rearview as Bradley's cruiser followed directly behind her. They all exited the cars at the same time and walked up the stairs to the front door.

Stanley opened the door before they had a chance to enter the code into the lock. "I didn't want you to knock and wake the kids," he said. "What took you so long?"

"Where's Rosie?" Bradley asked. "She needs to be in here for this conversation."

"I'm here, Bradley," said Rosie, getting up from her seat on the couch. "What's wrong?"

The three entered the room and, not bothering to take off their coats, moved to the chairs in the living room. "Why don't you sit back down?" he suggested. "And Stanley, why don't you sit down next to her?"

"What the hell...?" Stanley began to bluster.

"There was a shooting at the high school this evening," Mary said, interrupting him.

"What?" Rosie exclaimed. "Are you...? Is everyone fine?"

Bradley nodded. "Yes, but there were a couple of close calls," he said. "And if not for Ian's quick reflexes and Mary's training, things would have been a lot worse."

"Well, quite frankly, if the constable here hadn't shown up before we entered the school, Mary and I probably wouldn't be having this conversation with you," Ian added.

"But why would someone shoot at you?" Rosie asked.

Mary knelt down in front of Rosie and took her hands in her own. "The better question would be why would someone want to shoot at you?" Mary said pointedly. "They were expecting you and Ian, not me. And certainly not Bradley."

"Are you saying someone wanted to kill Rosie?" Stanley asked.

Mary nodded. "Or at least scare her away from the high school."

"But, but who?" Rosie asked, her face white with shock.

"That is what we intend to find out," Bradley said. "But in the meantime, we need to practice some precautions around here."

Stanley nodded, looping his arm around Rosie's shoulders and pulling her close. "I want her in protective custody," he said. "I want her in a safe house."

"Well, I agree with the sentiment, Stanley," Bradley said. "But it's going to be hard to prove this wasn't anything but us catching a petty thief off-guard."

"But the only one who knew she was gonna get the key was Gormley," Stanley said. "You could arrest him."

Rosie shook her head, slipped a hand out of Mary's grasp and patted Stanley's leg. "He's right, Stanley," she said. "Who is going to believe that I went to Gormley and asked for a key so I could investigate a ghost?"

"I'd believe you, Rosie," Bradley said with a smile. "But you're absolutely right, only those of us lucky to be in the Mary O'Reilly unit understand what's going on."

"So, what's gonna happen?" Stanley asked angrily. "You gonna leave her out there like a sitting duck?"

"You know better than that, Stanley," Mary chided. "You know we care about Rosie as much as you do."

Stanley grumbled. "Well, so what's your plan?"

"I want Rosie to stay with you for a few days," Bradley said. "This way she won't totally go off the radar and the people who tried to ambush her won't know that we've figured them out, so we'll have a better chance of catching them again. I can't think of anyone who would watch over her and protect her better than you."

"Darn right, ain't no one who would protect her better'n me," he spat.

Turning to her, he placed his hand over hers and squeezed it gently. "I promise you, Rosie, you'll be safe," he said. "Ain't no one gonna get to you with me standing in their way."

She laid her head down on his shoulder. "Oh, Stanley, I've never felt safer," she sighed.

He rose and pulled her up to her feet. "Are there things you need before you can stay at my house?" he asked.

"I would not advise going to your house tonight," Bradley said. "I don't know if they have someone there watching the place."

"Oh, dear, there are a few things that I really shouldn't be without," Rosie said. "But I don't want to risk...I do have my emergency kit back at the office, but I suspect you don't want me to go there either."

Bradley nodded. "Sorry, Rosie."

"Why don't you come upstairs with me?" Mary suggested. "I seem to recall you left some things here the last time you stayed."

The two women hurried up the stairs, their voices low as to not wake the children.

"Oh, Mary, I can't go to Stanley's without my makeup," she said. "I'll look like a hag in the morning and men aren't supposed to see women like that until after they're married."

Mary chuckled quietly. "Let's look through the guest bathroom and then through my bath and see if we can't put together enough supplies to make it through tomorrow morning."

In less than fifteen minutes Rosie had a bag packed and she was ready to go. With Stanley's arm

233

around her and her overnight case clasped at her chest, they said their good-nights and drove off to Stanley's home.

Mary closed the door behind them, a small smile on her face.

"So, care to share with us what was in that wee case?" Ian asked with a grin.

She shook her head. "Womanly secrets," she said.

He laughed. "Ah, it's just as well."

He turned to Bradley. "Do you think this house is in any danger?" he asked. "Seeing as Rosie used my name to get into the high school."

"I don't think so," he said. "She didn't tell them that you could speak with ghosts."

"Not that any ghost in their right mind could understand half of what he said," Mike quipped appearing in the room. "As Maggie puts it, he talks weird."

"Aye, but she loves me anyway," Ian added.

"Did you ever hear about Coach Thorne?" Mary asked.

"Oh, you mean the ghost coach?" Mike asked. "Yeah, he unlocked doors and opened windows in the chem lab. I was there once; I think it was the anniversary of the fire. We were all sitting in class when the front window started to open all by itself. It was so cool. Totally freaked the teacher out."

Ian chuckled. "Aye, I can understand that."

"Yeah, she decided she didn't want to teach chemistry any longer after that experience," he said.

"She was really a bad teacher anyway, so the coach did us a favor."

Mary laughed. "I wonder if he did it on purpose."

"So, you guys helping him?" Mike asked.

"Yeah, it looks like he has a good reason to be a ghost," Bradley said. "Someone planted a bomb in his room and the fire was a cover-up."

"Really, someone actually murdered the guy?"

Mary nodded. "Yeah, from the shots fired at us tonight, it looks like the murderer is still around and anxious for the crime to remain unsolved."

Mike looked at Mary. "I thought this was supposed to be a safe case," he scolded. "Do you not know the meaning of safe?"

Bradley chuckled, came up next to her and put his arm around her shoulders. "See. I'm not the only one."

"Well, I'm a bit more tired than I thought. I'm going to call it a night," Ian said, deciding it was time to leave Mary and Bradley alone. "Come upstairs with me Mike and tell me more about your high school days. I need something to help me fall asleep quickly."

"Oh, funny," Mike said, gliding up beside him. "And I suppose your high school days were any better."

"A might better than yours, I'd gather," he replied.

Mary leaned back against Bradley and giggled. "They are so cute together," she laughed.

Bradley turned her toward him, held her loosely in his arms and lowered his forehead to hers. "My heart stopped beating when I heard that second shot," he said. "I thought…"

She lifted her hands and cradled his face. "The same thing I thought when I saw him behind you and heard the first shot."

He nodded. "Which was?" he encouraged.

"Crap, he'll do anything to get out of a date."

He chuckled softly, pulled her closer and kissed her on the side of her neck. "You're still planning on wearing that little black dress, right?" he whispered in her ear, sending a quiver of excitement through her.

"Ummm, hmmm," she breathed slowly as he continued to place small kisses against the side of her neck. "And sexy black heels with black silk stockings."

He paused mid-kiss. "They wouldn't have a seam up the back of them, would they?"

She grinned. "All the way up the back of them."

He drew back and looked at her face, her grin wide and her eyes sparkling. "There is no way in hell I'm missing this date," he said, and pulled her close for a bone-melting kiss.

# Chapter Thirty-nine

"What the hell were you thinking?" Walter Gormley shouted, spittle gathering at the corners of his mouth. "I just got off the phone with the police. You went into one of my schools and shot at someone. Do you realize what you could have done?"

"Yes, I could have gotten rid of a problem that could ruin all of our lives," Ephraim Brandlocker said. "And don't tell me what to do, Gormley. I put you in that position and I can just as easily take you out."

This time the bar was closed and the shades were drawn, so no one walking past the tavern would be able to tell anyone was inside.

"It was a prank, right?" Walter asked, trying to read Ephraim's face. "You told me it would just be a prank. Something to make my dad look better and put a little egg on Thorne's face."

Ephraim nodded. "That's what I told you all right."

"So, what's the big deal? It was a stupid prank and it went wrong, that's all. We were teenagers, it won't be held against us anymore. There's a two-year statute of limitations on wrongful death, I looked it up."

Ephraim laughed bitterly. "Listen, Wally, there isn't a statute of limitations on murder."

Wally fell back in his chair. "What? This wasn't murder," he said. "The chemicals I put in the beakers just caused the fire. It got out of control, yeah, but we didn't do anything to hurt anyone."

Ephraim laughed again. "That's why I like you, Wally," he said. "You've always been so gullible, so easy to manipulate. Yeah, the chemicals didn't cause the explosion, but the bomb I set under his desk sure did."

There was a moment of shocked silence.

"You didn't say anything about a bomb," Wally said, his voice hoarse with shock. "You never said anything about a bomb."

Ephraim shrugged and sat back against his chair. "That's what you say now," he said. "But as I recall, it was your idea. You came to me wanting to get back at the teacher who was going to steal your dad's tenure. Of course, since all the evidence is gone, it would be my word against yours. And, since Rosie got shot at after you gave her the keys, I wonder who they are going to believe."

"You can't do this. They won't believe you," Walter stammered. "Why would I…?"

"Changed your life when your dad became head of the Chemistry Department, didn't it, Wally?" he sneered. "More money, more prestige and instead of going to a community college you actually got to go downstate. Yes, I'd say that was worth killing for."

"I didn't kill him," Wally screamed.

Ephraim laughed softly. "Yeah, tell that to the judge."

Wally dropped his head into his hands and cried. "Oh, God, I didn't do it. I can't go to jail."

"Yeah, you wouldn't last a long time in jail, Wally," he agreed. "You're just too weak. You know what they do to guys like you in jail."

Wally felt sick to his stomach.

"But, Wally, you don't have to go to jail," Ephraim said calmly.

Wally looked up at him, his face red and blotchy, snot running from his nose and his face wet with a mixture of tears and sweat. "I don't?" he asked, running a sleeve across his face.

Ephraim leaned forward toward Wally. "No, Wally, all you got to do is make sure Rosie Meriwether stays quiet. Forever."

# Chapter Forty

The next morning Mary entered the private nursing home that sat along the border of one of Freeport's finest parks. Even though the facilities were built more than seventy years ago, they remained in pristine condition, the grand lady of nursing homes in the area.

She walked across the Oriental rug placed over the polished wood floor and smiled at the receptionist seated behind the desk. The name plate on the top of the desk read "Jennika Nikole." "Good morning, Jennika," she said. "I'm here to see Ross Gormley. Is he still in his room?"

Mary had learned when she was a rookie cop to never give someone a chance to turn you down, so she never asked permission to see someone, but assumed she could and skipped to the next question.

Jennika looked down at a schedule and smiled up at Mary. "No, Ross is in the All-Purpose Room right now," she said. "It's down to the end of the hall and then turn left."

"Thank you," Mary responded and followed the directions.

The All-Purpose Room was comfortably furnished with a grand piano in one corner, bookshelf and occasional chairs in another and a number of small card tables scattered throughout the room. A grouping of picture windows looked out to a statuary garden that was beautiful even in February. In front of the windows was a man seated in a wheelchair.

As she approached, she saw that he was dressed in a button down shirt and khaki pants, his face was clean shaven and his hair tidy. In one hand he held a paperback book, his other hand was clasping his pant leg tightly.

Mary approached him. "Hello, are you Mr. Gormley?"

The man seemed startled for a moment, but once he looked up and saw Mary's face he smiled. "You're Patrice Stewart, aren't you?" he said with a broad smile. "I never forget one of my students."

He put the book down and held out his left hand; Mary took it in both of her hands and shook it gently. "Can't do a damned thing with my other hand," he said. "Hope you don't mind."

"No, I don't mind at all. Actually, my name is Mary O'Reilly," she confessed, pulling up a folding chair and sitting across from him. "May I visit with you for a little bit?"

"Of course, Patrice, of course," he said. "How is your family?"

She grinned. "They are wonderful," she said. "And how is yours?"

He shrugged. "Well, you know Wally, always too busy to visit," he said. "Do you know what I really think?"

Mary shook her head. "No, what?"

"I don't think I was the father he wanted me to be," he said.

"Oh, no," she replied. "He's probably just busy with his job."

Ross shrugged. "The boy has been busy since high school. He changed in high school, don't know what it was. We used to be so close."

"Speaking of high school, I was wondering if we could talk about Charles Thorne," she said. "Do you remember him?"

He smiled and nodded his head slowly. "Now, Charlie, there was a great man," he said. "The good ones always die too young."

"Do you remember when he died?" she asked.

"I do remember," he said, pulling a handkerchief out of his pocket and wiping his eyes. "Changed my life forever."

"In what way?" Mary asked.

"Charlie and me, we worked together in the Chemistry Department," he said. "But you're too young to remember those days. Me and Charlie were both married, both had families. But Charlie, he was the up-and-coming star. He was a coach, he was a great teacher and he had a way of connecting with those kids..."

He looked up at her. "He got them to love chemistry," he said, shaking his head. "I always thought chemistry was something to drill into their thick skulls." He chuckled and shook his head. "But when I heard laughter coming from the next room I was amazed."

He stared at her for a moment and seemed to lose his train of thought. "Did you have Charlie as a teacher?" he asked.

"No," she replied kindly. "No, I never had the pleasure."

"He had a way of teaching about displacement," he laughed out loud. "Raquel Welch displacement theory, he called it. I thought it was silly, taking a serious area of study and making fun of it. But damn if his kids didn't get better grades on all their finals than mine."

"How did that make you feel?" Mary asked.

"Nervous as hell," he said. "Here's this upstart who's doing better than me. The kids are dropping my class to get into his. I wanted to put a stop to it."

Mary sat forward in her chair. "So, what did you do?" she asked.

"I went over to his classroom one morning, before school started," he said. "I grabbed the doorknob, but my hand wouldn't close. It wouldn't do what I wanted it to do. It was just shaking."

He put his left hand on top of the right one.

"Charlie took me by the arm and pulled me into his room," he continued. "I looked up at him, and I was scared, really scared. He asked me how long it'd been happening. I told him off and on for a couple of years, but only for a moment, nothing like this."

"So, what did he do?" Mary asked.

Ross wiped his eyes again with his handkerchief and took a deep breath. "He put his arm around me and told me that we'd work it out," he said. "He told me he had a plan."

Mary wiped a stray tear from her cheek.

"He sounds like a good guy," she said.

"He saved my job," Ross whispered. "He'd come in early in the morning or stay late and prepare the experiments for both of our classes. He trained student Chemistry Captains and gave them extra credit to help in my classroom. No one knew, not for a long time, and by the time they found out, I'd been tenured and my job was safe."

"By then Charlie was dead," she said.

"Yeah, I know Charlie would have gotten that tenure, and he deserved it," he said. "I welcomed him being head of the department because I also knew he'd protect me. And I sure didn't want to have to go to conventions and speak, not with the Parkinson's."

"So, Charlie's death didn't help you?" she asked.

He shook his head. "No, I called in sick half the time between his death and the tenure decision," he said. "And, to be honest, I was sick. My good friend was dead and I hadn't been able to get anyone to listen to the truth about it."

"What?" Mary asked.

"After the fire, I found out that one of my beakers had been tampered with too," he said. "Since Charlie prepared them both the night before, I took half of them to my lab. My senior class was later than

Charlie's so we never got to do the experiments. When I heard it was beakers that exploded I tested them and found a chemical in it that Charlie wouldn't have added to it. But there wasn't enough in any of them for an explosion."

"You told the authorities?" Mary asked.

He shook his head. "Yes, I told them, but no one wanted to listen. Those investigators they brought in, they had their answers before they even started. So, I decided maybe I needed to do a little investigation of my own."

"You did an investigation?" she asked.

He nodded. "Got all kinds of evidence. Figured someday someone would come looking, wanting to know the truth."

"Well, Mr. Gormley, today is that day."

# Chapter Forty-one

Mary walked up the steps to the second floor of City Hall and hurried to Bradley's office. "Hi Dorothy," she said to his assistant. "Is Bradley in?"

Dorothy nodded. "Yes, he's looking through some old reports," she said. "You can go on in."

"Good morning," she said, softly closing the door behind her.

He looked up from the report and a smile spread across his face. "Morning," he said. "So, have you solved the case yet?"

She shook her head. "No, but I think I can cross at least one name off the suspect list."

"Who?"

"I met with Ross Gormley this morning," she said, sitting on the edge of his desk. "He didn't kill Charlie. He had nothing to gain and everything to lose."

"Did his son know that?" Bradley asked.

Mary shook her head. "No, I don't think so," she said.

He closed the file and pushed it to the side of his desk. "You know what the problem is?" he asked.

She shook her head. "No, what's the problem?"

He motioned her closer. "I really think we need to be careful about who hears this," he said, lowering his voice and leaning across his desk.

Moving closer, she asked anxiously, "What is it?"

Shaking his head, he leaned even further across the desk, so she could feel his breath on her face. "Every time I start reading these reports, a mental image of you in silk stockings and a black dress pops into my head and I'm useless."

She bit her lower lip to contain the laughter. 'Oh, I'm terribly sorry," she lied.

He reached up, slid his hand around her neck and pulled her even closer. "Yeah, well, I'm not," he said, reaching up and kissing her.

A discreet knock on the door had them pulling apart like guilty teenagers. Mary jumped off the desk and was already standing next to the window when Dorothy came through the door with a handful of files.

"Thank you, Dorothy," Bradley said, clearing his throat. "Is there anything else?"

Dorothy seemed to be having a difficult time schooling her features into the professional reserve she usually maintained. "Well, sir," she said. "I think it might be beneficial if you move the mobile intercom from where you have it on your desk."

"I'm sorry?" Bradley asked, looking at the metal box sitting below him on the desk.

"Well, sir, when you lean forward on your desk, you inadvertently press the button," she said.

Bradley looked down at the button, over at Mary and his face began to slowly turn red. "When I lean forward I accidentally press the intercom button," he repeated. "And perhaps that recently happened?"

Dorothy nodded. "And I must say that most of the officers online agree that Miss O'Reilly dressed in silk stockings and a black dress would be distracting to them too."

Mary clapped her hand over her mouth and turned to the window.

Bradley loosened his shirt collar. "Thank you, Dorothy, I appreciate your advice," he said, picking up the intercom and moving it to the other side of his desk. "And I appreciate your quick intervention."

Then he smiled at Mary. "And for the record, even without silk stockings she is quite distracting."

Once the door closed Mary dissolved into a fit of laughter. "Oh, Bradley, I am so sorry," she chortled. "But you should have seen your face."

He didn't say a word, just met her eyes, slowly stood up and walked away from his desk. Their eyes locked, he moved next to her, reached past her and systematically closed all of the blinds. Then reaching backwards, he pressed the button on the intercom. "Dorothy, I'm going to kiss Miss O'Reilly now, do I have an all clear?"

He heard his assistant giggle. "Yes, sir, you do."

"Go Chief!" one of his officers called, followed by a chorus of whistles and encouragement.

He lifted his finger from the button and slipped his hands up Mary's arms, finally cradling her face in his hands. "Do I have the all clear, Miss O'Reilly?" he whispered.

"Yes," she breathed. "Yes, you do."

He angled his face and brushed his lips against hers. She moaned softly and he captured it in his mouth. "Mary," he sighed and crushed his lips against hers.

# Chapter Forty-two

Ian looked up from his computer when the front door opened and Mary and Bradley entered carrying several large boxes. "Well, welcome," he said. "And to what do I owe the pleasure of your company?"

"Bradley thought working from here would be less distracting," Mary said, with a grin. "Besides, I want to see how brilliant you really are."

They placed the boxes on the kitchen table and Ian followed them.

"And what do we have here?" he asked.

"A legacy of friendship," Mary replied, taking the top off the first box. "These are samples, photos and notes about the explosion from Ross Gormley."

"What?" Ian asked, pulling the top off the next box.

"Ross didn't think it was an accident, so he did his own investigation," Mary explained. "When the authorities wouldn't listen to him, he carefully catalogued it all, hoping one day someone would ask the right questions."

Ian picked up a glass slide and looked at it. "Great, but how are we supposed to study these…"

Mary opened a third box and pulled out a microscope. "It's not fancy," she said. "But I hope it will do the trick."

"Aye, it'll be fine," Ian said, glancing through the notes. "It looks like he put this information together so it was thorough enough to hold up in a court of law. The man's brilliant."

Two hours later, Ian looked up from his stack of papers and shook his head. "He even has pieces of wire that were taped to the floor that ran back to the detonator."

"So, someone was watching to see when the last student got out and then ignited the bomb," Mary said.

"So, who is our prime suspect?" Bradley asked. "We've got a lot of evidence, but do we have a name?"

"Well, chemicals and cover ups come from our good friends at B&R," Ian said.

"Yeah, but why?" Mary asked. "What would they have against Coach Thorne?"

The door opened and Rosie and Stanley came in. "I took the long away around," Stanley said. "I don't think anyone followed me."

"Since I couldn't go to my place, we stopped by the Historical Society and borrowed a yearbook from the year Coach Thorne died," Rosie said. "I thought it would be helpful."

She opened the book up on the table and turned to the photo of her class.

"Wow, Walter is a different person," Bradley said.

"Really, what's different?" Mary asked.

"He's about four times that size now," Rosie said. "He doesn't look healthy at all."

Mary told them about the conversation she had with Walter's father.

"I wonder if Walter realized just how much Coach Thorne did for his father," Rosie mused.

"Probably not," Stanley said. "Ain't something a dad would want to share with his teenaged son."

"Oh, there's your friend, Stevo," Mary said, scanning the photo. "But I don't see his wife, Lo."

"Oh, she wasn't in our class," Rosie said. "She was in the class below ours."

"She wasn't in the chemistry class when the fire occurred?" Mary asked.

Rosie shook her head. "No, she didn't have it until the following year."

"I'd like to visit with Lo Morris," Mary said. "She said something that's been bothering me. I don't think I'll be very long, Rosie, would you stay here and wait for the children?"

"Oh, I'd love too," she said. "I'll make more cookies."

"Oh, Rosie," Ian said. "Bless you."

"If it's alright with you," Bradley said. "I'd like to bring this evidence to the lab and get it tested. Ian would you mind giving me a hand?"

"No, I'd love to hear what the fellows at the lab think of it," he said, slipping into his coat.

"Well, iffen you all think it's fine, I'd like to stop by and talk with Caleb Brandlocker," Stanley said. "He suffered a stroke a while back, he's over in the nursing home."

"Rosie, what do you think?" Mary asked. "I can stay."

Rosie shook her head.

"Don't be silly," she said. "Who would know I was here?"

Stanley leaned forward and gave her a kiss on the cheek. "You lock that door once we all leave, hear?"

She giggled. "Yes, dear."

# Chapter Forty-three

Caleb Brandlocker was in the private care wing of the nursing home. He had a small room that was a cross between a hospital room and a residence. On his good days he could get himself up and around, but those days seemed to get farther and farther apart.

Stanley knocked on his door. "Caleb, you taking visitors? It's me, Stanley Wagner."

"Stanley, come in, come in," Caleb said hoarsely, his voice barely a whisper. "How are you?"

Stanley walked across the room and shook Caleb's hand which was thin and frail, very different from the robust businessman who would visit the stationary store when Stanley was running things.

"I can't complain, Caleb," Stanley said. "I got my kids running the store, time on my hands and I'm getting myself a pretty new wife in about a month."

Caleb smiled. "You old dog, you," he said. "A new wife. Ain't you too old for that?"

"Never too old to fall in love, Caleb," Stanley said. "And I seen some pretty cute little nurses out there, you ought to try dating 'em."

Caleb's wheezing laughter filled the room for a few minutes and Stanley was happy to see some of the worry lines relax on his face. Finally, after a bout or two of coughing, Caleb was able to speak. "You're a good man, Stanley," he said. "And you got a fine family. I envy you."

"Well, hell, Caleb," Stanley said. "I just saw your boy the other day, looks like he could run in the Olympics. He seems to be doing a fine job running your business."

Caleb shook his head. "I made mistakes raising that boy," he admitted. "Thought too highly of him. Made him think he was better, more important than anyone else. Made him think he could have anything he wanted."

"Nothing wrong with ambition," Stanley said.

Caleb's hand snaked over to Stanley's and he held it. "Not ambition," he said. "Cruelty. The boy's got bad blood."

Stanley's blood ran cold. "Caleb, I don't want to disrespect you, but I got to ask you a question. My fiancée, Rosie, she's got someone trying to hurt her because she was looking into the death of Coach Thorne. Did your boy have anything to do with that?"

# Chapter Forty-four

Bradley and Ian were the last ones to leave and Rosie locked the door firmly behind them. She turned on the television and headed to the kitchen to pull out the baking supplies. A cooking show was demonstrating a new way to bake oatmeal cookies.

"Well, oatmeal cookies," she said, "that's just the thing."

Opening the pantry door, she looked up and saw that Stanley had stored the flour canister back up on the top shelf. She glanced up and decided it really wasn't all that high. Standing on her tiptoes, she reached up for the canister. She could just barely touch it with her fingertips. Sliding her fingers alongside it, she slowly moved it forward. Placing three fingertips on the bottom to hold it upright, she stretched and pushed it forward with the other hand. The canister teetered on the edge of the shelf and fell forward.

POOF!

Rosie couldn't believe it. She was covered in flour, the floor was covered in flour and the shelves were covered in flour. She stamped her foot, causing another cloud of flour. "Well, well, well," she sputtered, then looked around to be sure no one could hear her and let loose. "Damn!"

Picking up the whisk brush, she figured she ought to get herself cleaned off first. Carefully, trying to avoid getting flour on anything else, she made her way across the kitchen floor and opened the backdoor. She stepped out on the porch.

"Hello, Rosie."

Rosie screamed. She tried to run back into the house, but Walter grabbed her arm and she couldn't move. He placed a strip of duct tape over her mouth and pulled her to him. "I'm sorry, Rosie, I really didn't want to do this, but I don't want to go to jail."

He pulled her arms around her and wrapped duct tape around them. Then he led her down the porch stairs and through the yard to his van, waiting behind the house. "Quite frankly, I never thought it would be this easy. Thank you, Rosie," he said.

*Chapter Forty-five*

Mary parked in front of the Morris's house and hurried up the sidewalk. She had a funny feeling in the pit of her stomach and wanted to talk to Lo and get back to Rosie.

She waited for only a moment after ringing the bell and Lo answered the door. "Hi, I'm Rosie's friend, Mary," she said.

"Of course, I remember you," she replied. "Won't you come in?"

Mary followed Lo into a comfortably appointed home furnished in the colors of autumn; warm and bright. They walked into the living room and Mary sat on a large wheat-colored couch across from Lo. "I was thinking about something you said regarding Coach Thorne," Mary said. "And I want to ask you about it."

Lo nodded.

"You said he saved many lives and he didn't care if you were rich and powerful or just one of the little guys," she said. "I got the feeling there was more to what you were saying than just that. I wouldn't ask you if it wasn't important, but I need you to tell me what happened."

Lo shook her head. "He's been dead for forty years," she said. "Why even bother? Who is it going to help?"

"Last night someone shot at me," Mary explained. "But they thought I was Rosie."

"Oh, no," Lo gasped. "Is everyone fine?"

Mary nodded. "For now," she said. "But now that we started investigating we can't stop until we find out what happened. For Rosie's sake."

Lo nodded slowly and clasped her hands together. "Brandlocker," she whispered. "Ephraim Brandlocker. He was a senior and I was a sophomore. His parents were wealthy beyond my imagination and my parents, well, we were not wealthy. He picked me up in his car and took me to nice restaurants. He was nice to me; at least I thought he was being nice to me."

"What happened?"

"He was on the Varsity baseball team," she said. "He was a pitcher and he was one of their best homerun hitters too. His dad said he was going to the majors."

Mary remembered what Charlie said about parents who thought their children were cut out for the big league.

"So, what happened?"

"They just won a big game," she said. "They were going to the Division Finals. Ephraim asked me to wait for him. He went into the locker room with the other guys and I waited by the bleachers for him. By the time he came out it was getting dark and the bleachers were deserted. I told him I needed to go home. But he told me he wanted to celebrate."

She shuddered and wrapped her arms around herself.

"I told him I couldn't stay and he pushed me into the bleachers. He said I didn't understand; I was going to be his celebration. I screamed and he put his hand over my mouth. He told me that no one would believe I didn't want to have sex with him. That no one would believe the poor girl. That his father would ruin my family if I didn't…cooperate."

Lo stood up and walked to the other end of the room. "I kept shaking my head and crying. He pushed me down on one of the seats and started to climb over me," she took a deep breath. "That's when Coach Thorne grabbed him by the back of the neck and threw him onto the ground. He grabbed his shirt and pushed him up against the building. He told him if he ever heard of him doing something like this again, he would not only be expelled, he'd be arrested."

"What happened to Ephraim?"

She shook her head. "Money does buy everything," she said, "especially in a small town. Coach tried to get him suspended, but the school board wouldn't allow it. He tried to get some disciplinary action against him, but nothing ever happened. He even tried to kick him off the team, but the school wouldn't let him do it. But the one thing he could do was bench him. Ephraim never played another game with the team. He ended up going to a Junior College and never got a baseball scholarship. He blamed the coach."

"Blamed him enough to kill him?" Mary asked.

Lo nodded. "Ephraim had a lot of anger," she said. "And no one ever told him no. No one except Coach Thorne."

"Did you ever try to press charges?"

"I left town and moved in with my aunt for the rest of my sophomore year and my junior year," she said. "My family thought it would be best for me to be gone."

"Why?"

Lo turned back and looked at Mary. "When we were dating, Ephraim would bring me to his father's fertilizer plant, out on Henderson Road," she said. "There were huge bins with giant augers that would mix and crush the ingredients together. Ephraim liked catching small animals and throwing them into the bin, just to watch them die. That's the kind of person he was. That's why my parents sent me out of town."

"That explains a lot of things," she said. "Thank you for telling me."

"Please, don't let Stevo know," she said. "Even after all these years, he might be angry…"

Mary nodded. "I understand," she said. "I won't let him know."

Mary hurried out to the car; the feeling in the pit of her stomach was growing stronger. She nearly jumped when her phone rang.

"Hello?"

"Mary, it's Ian," he said. "Rosie's gone."

# Chapter Forty-six

Rosie lay on the back floor of the panel van on a pile of old moving blankets.

*This is so unsanitary. And what is he thinking? There are no seat belts back here! If we were to get into an accident, I could be thrown from this vehicle and killed.*

Killed.

*Walter wants to kill me. Well, I'm never going to date him now, even if he asked nicely.*

*That's ridiculous, stop thinking silly thoughts, you're engaged now. You can't date other men anyway.*

Stanley.

*If I die I can't marry Stanley. I love Stanley. And I think I've found the perfect dress. Mary wouldn't get herself in a situation like this. Mary would have kicked their butts.* She gave her head a little shake. *No, Mary would have kicked their asses. There I thought it – asses.*

*What would Mary do?*

She looked around the van, but there really didn't seem to be a good way to escape, especially since it was moving and her hands were tied. She twisted her wrists; the tape wasn't sticking very well. It must have been the flour. She wriggled her arms back and forth and the duct tape loosened even more. Soon she was able to slip one of her hands out.

*I'm channeling Mary. I can do this.*

She was jolted around when the van stopped. Remembering Walter shouldn't know about her hands, she stuck them back together and waited for him to open the door.

The van door opened and Rosie could see a loading dock. She could see by the collection of weeds and brush overgrowing the area that it hadn't been used for a long time. Walter reached in and helped her out of the van and the he ripped the duct tape off her mouth and she winced.

*That hurt!*

"I'm real sorry, Rosie," Walter repeated. "If you had just not seen that ghost…"

*How would Mary answer him?*

"Did you know that Coach Thorne saved your dad's job?" Rosie asked, trying not to shiver in the cold wind.

Walter stopped and shook his head. "No, he was preventing my dad from getting tenure."

"No, he was covering up for your dad because of the Parkinson's. Your dad was afraid he was going to get fired," Rosie said. "Coach Thorne stayed late or came in early so he could put together the experiments for your dad's classes."

Walter shook his head. "No, that can't be true."

"Come on, Wally, you remember when your dad got Parkinson's," Rosie said. "You must have known there was no way he could measure chemicals for the experiments. Your life would have been ruined without Coach Thorne."

Walter grabbed Rosie's arm and pulled her up the ramp and into the warehouse. "I won't listen to you," he said.

She quickly looked around. The warehouse was nearly empty. There were some pieces of broken wooden pallets scattered around, a rusted dumpster with pipes, cardboard and lumber overflowing from it and a number of white plastic fifty-five gallon barrels that looked fairly new.

"You won't listen to me because you know I'm right," she said, pulling away from him toward the dumpster. "Don't be a coward, Wally, at least admit that."

Walter was breathing heavy, sweat rolling on his forehead, when he stopped and looked at Rosie. "Maybe it's true and maybe you're right," he said. "But there's nothing I can do about it now. My hands are tied."

She slipped one hand out of the duct tape. "Well, mine aren't," she yelled, grabbing one of the pipes and swinging it toward Walter.

The pipe swung forward, but then stopped. Rosie looked over her shoulder and saw a tall man had caught the end of the pipe.

"He's trying to hurt me," Rosie said, struggling to pull the pipe out of the man's hands. "You have to let go."

"Wally, will you please take control of this situation?" Ephraim ordered, ripping the pipe out of her hands.

Wally grabbed both of Rosie's arms from behind and held her. "What do you want me to do?"

Ephraim smiled and walked over to electrical box and flipped the switch. "We're going to allow our friend Rosie to get closer to nature," he said softly, walking to another control panel.

He pressed a button and a harsh mechanical noise vibrated the building. "I apologize," he said. "It does get a little loud. It's our auger. We use it for making fertilizer. An amazing piece of equipment; not only does it mix and grind material together, but it also pulls them up a metal shaft filled with stainless steel blades to ensure the pieces are microscopic."

He looked at Rosie. "Unfortunately, pieces that are too big to fit in the shaft get hacked up into smaller, less..." he paused, "...noticeable pieces of material."

Walking closer to her, he ran a finger across her cheek and she moved her face. "I remember one of the first times I saw it in use, I was fascinated," he said. "A rat had slipped into the bin and couldn't get out. I watched as it was pulled closer and closer to the blades. It was mesmerizing."

He looked at her, his eyes bright with enjoyment. "Finally it was caught, the blade ripped it up in a matter of seconds and the blood just mixed with the rest of the minerals."

He chuckled. "Extra protein, that's what my dad called it, extra protein."

"This can't be real," Rosie whispered. "This doesn't happen in the real world."

She tried to look over her shoulder. "Wally, you can't let him do this. I can't die, I'm getting married."

"I'm sorry Rosie," Walter said. "I don't have a choice."

# Chapter Forty-seven

Stanley's phone rang and he stopped his conversation with Caleb to answer it.

"Hello," he said.

"They've taken Rosie," Mary said.

Stanley felt his heart drop to his feet and he looked at the old man in front of him. "Caleb," he said, his voice shaking. "They've taken my Rosie. They're going to hurt her. You've got to tell me..."

"Stanley, you don't know," Caleb said. "You're not sure."

"Caleb, I remember your wife and how much you loved her," he said. "I love my Rosie. She's my life. Please don't cover up for him this time. Please."

Caleb closed his eyes and bowed his head. "The fertilizer plant," Caleb said. "On Henderson."

"Mary, the fertilizer plant," Stanley repeated, his voice shaking.

"Already on my way," she said. "Tell Bradley."

Stanley stood up on shaky legs. "I gotta go, Caleb," he said. "I gotta go find my Rosie."

"Godspeed," Caleb whispered. "Godspeed."

Stanley ran down the hall, toward the door to the parking lot. He pulled his keys out of his pocket when his phone rang again.

"Yes?" he yelled into the phone.

"Stanley, it's Bradley."

"They've taken her to the fertilizer plant," he cried. "You don't know what he does out there."

"Ian's on his way to get you," Bradley said. "He'll be there in a minute. I'm going to the plant."

"Hurry, Bradley," Stanley whispered, after Bradley had ended the call. "Hurry."

# Chapter Forty-eight

Mary shifted the Roadster into fifth gear and whipped onto Henderson Road. The dust from the gravel blew a cloud behind her car as she increased her speed. *Not Rosie, not Rosie*, she prayed.

She nearly missed the entrance to the old plant, but sent the Roadster skidding in a curve and then punched the accelerator feeling it bite down on the gravel and jump forward. She drove over to the loading dock, threw the car into park and ran up the ramp into the warehouse.

"Mary!"

Mary looked up in the direction of Rosie's scream and saw her on a metal catwalk two floors up that led to a giant steel bin, her arms caught in Walter's grasp. "Give up now, Walter," she yelled over the din from the auger. "The police are on the way."

She started to run to the stairs that led to Rosie when her legs were knocked out from under her. She fell hard and landed on her back, the breath knocked out of her.

The floor was cold and damp against her back and the room was filled with shadows. The warehouse moved out of focus, and suddenly she was back in the basement.

Ephraim stood over her, but all she could see was Gary.

"What do we have here?" he asked. He knelt down and leaned over her. "So nice of you to drop in."

He ran his hand across her cheek. "Very nice of you to drop in."

Mary felt her stomach contract and the panic set in once again. She was trapped. "Please," she cried. "Please, don't hurt me."

"Oh, sweetheart, I won't hurt you," he whispered, kneeling over her. "At least not much."

"Mary," Rosie screamed. "Help me."

"She can't help you, Rosie," he taunted. "She can't even help herself."

*Rosie needs me,* she thought. *Rosie's in danger. I have to help Rosie.*

She could hear Ian's voice in her head. *"You have to help yourself, darling, give him what for."*

Gary wasn't going to win. She fought him last time and won. She could do it again.

Mary brought her knee up and crushed into his groin. He screamed in pain. She yelled with power.

She reached over and grabbed the piece of wood he used on her. He rolled on top of her and tried to wrestle it from her grasp. She fought against him, rolling on the concrete floor. She elbowed him in the solar plexus and he gasped in pain. She pulled the wood out of his hands and smashed it against his head.

He rolled away and pulled himself up on his feet. Breathing heavy, he ran at her.

"I'll teach you to fight with me, bitch," he screamed.

Mary rolled on her back, and feigned fear, while she brought her knees up toward her chest. When he got close enough, using both feet, she kicked up and out, catching him in the stomach and sending him crashing back into the dumpster.

She jumped to her feet, walked across the room and kicked him again.

"Walter, help me," he cried out.

"No. No! I'm getting out of here," Walter yelled, releasing Rosie and running in the opposite direction.

Undeterred from the object of her wrath, Mary grabbed a heavy piece of lumber from the dumpster. She swung it sideways with all her might and hit Ephraim in the shoulder. He screamed and tried to crawl away from her.

"Stop," he shrieked. "I beg of you, stop."

She walked over, straddled his body and glared down at him. "You are not going to hurt me again," she vowed. "You are never going to hurt anyone again."

Then she lifted the piece of lumber over her head.

"Mary, stop," Bradley said, putting his hand on the piece of wood. "He can't hurt you anymore."

Mary jerked to her side, ready to defend herself.

"Mary, it's me, Bradley," he said calmly. "You did it. You won."

It took her a moment, but Bradley could see the moment she snapped out of her flashback. She released her grasp on the wood and stepped away from the man on the floor.

"Bradley, I..." she whispered, holding her hand over her mouth. "I thought he was Gary. I was fighting Gary."

"Yeah, you did a hell of a job. Are you okay?"

She nodded slowly and then turned toward the stairs. "Rosie?"

Rosie was across the room in Stanley's arms.

"Is she okay?" Mary asked.

"Yeah," Bradley said. "Thanks to you."

"Me?"

"You scared the hell of Walter," Bradley said. "He came running out of the plant. Unfortunately for Walter, Stanley and Ian had just arrived. Stanley took Walter down with one punch to the jaw. He would have done more, but Ian held him back."

"Bradley, I went a little crazy," she said. "I couldn't let him win."

"No, you couldn't," he said, pulling her into his arms and holding her while the paramedics took Ephraim away. "And you saved Rosie's life."

She put her head on his shoulder and then looked up. "Where are the kids?"

"I sent Ashley Deutsch over to wait for them," he said. "She's great with kids."

She reached up and kissed him. "Thank you."

"Ready to go home?" he asked. "I want you to get a good night's sleep tonight."

"Why?"

He grinned and kissed her softly. "You have a hot date tomorrow night," he said.

She smiled. "That's right; I don't know how I could have forgotten. But we have one stop first."

## Chapter Forty-nine

School had just ended for the week. The janitors were making their ways down the halls, pushing their brooms and picking up the trash that had been left behind. A few teachers stood and spoke with each other in the hall, as Mary, Ian and Bradley made their way to the chemistry lab.

"I still think Rosie should have come with us," Mary said.

"All she wanted to do was go back to your place and clean up the mess on the floor," Bradley said.

Mary looked up, alarmed.

"Don't worry, Ashley and the kids already had it handled," he reassured her. "They have orders to sit her down and get her a cup of tea."

"Did you hear what she said about channeling you?" Ian asked. "She nearly had Walter down. I'm hoping it doesn't ruin her."

"And what do you mean by that?" she asked.

"Well, if she's channeling you, will she still be able to bake?" he asked. "Aye, she'll be the toughest real estate broker in the city, but really, what's more important?"

Bradley chuckled. "And what is more important, Ian?"

"We'll have to pick up more flour on the way home," Ian said, after a moment. "And perhaps a new canister."

Chuckling, Mary shook her head at him. "Perhaps you ought to make some cookies for us," she said. "Good Scottish shortbread."

"I would, Mary, I really would," Ian replied. "But I don't want to hurt poor Rosie's feelings."

They let themselves into the chemistry lab. Mary took Bradley's hand and they waited for a moment until Charlie materialized.

"We wanted to let you know we found out Ephraim Brandlocker murdered you," Mary said. "He placed a bomb under your desk and waited until the last student was out before he detonated it."

"Aye, and your friend Ross Gormley tried to tell the authorities years ago that it wasn't an accident, but no one would listen," Ian added. "He still put together an evidence trail that will help the officials put Ephraim away for a long time."

Charlie shook his head. "That's amazing," he said. "Why would he do that?"

"Lo thought it was because you told him no," she said. "You had the courage to stop him."

"Well, thanks," Charlie said. "Thanks for letting me know."

Mary looked around. "Charlie, don't you feel any differently?" she asked.

He shrugged. "Um, no, like what?"

"Like your unfinished business has been resolved," Ian said.

"No. No, I feel pretty much like I felt for the past forty years or so," he said. "Dead."

"Well, there must be something else," she said and then she smiled slowly. "That's it."

"What are you talking about?" he asked.

"Don't go away," she said. "I'll be back tomorrow."

"Really, Mary, I'm not planning on going anywhere."

The next afternoon, the door to the chemistry room opened and the small group made their way inside. They set up a small display at the front of the room and then waited.

"Is he here?" Lo asked.

Mary shook her head. "No, not yet."

Stevo peered into the shadows at the back of the room. "I thought I saw something."

Mary smiled. "No, really, nothing yet."

"I know what will do it," Rosie said, lighting a candle and placing it in the middle of the table.

Immediately a soft wind blew the candle out and most of the occupants of the room shivered. Mary watched Charlie materialize next to her. "I told you I'd be back," she said. "Last night when we told you about Ephraim and you stayed, I realized perhaps you might still have some other unfinished business."

She pointed to the other people in the room. "So we gathered a big group together to see what we could do about it. You might not recognize these people, but they are your former students Rosie Meriwether, Stevo Morris and Lo…"

"Lo Johnson," she supplied. "I was never your student, but I will never forget what you did for me."

He smiled. "I remember them all."

"He remembers all of you," Mary said.

"Coach, we just wanted to let you know how much..." Stevo's voice cracked and he wiped away a tear. "How much we loved you. How much you meant in our lives and how we never forgot you."

Lo slipped her arm around Stevo and nodded. "We named our first son Charlie," she said. "We bought him a chemistry set when he was ten," she giggled. "...and he nearly burned the house down."

"Performs chemistry like his father," Charlie said.

Mary chuckled. "Charlie said your son performs chemistry like his father."

Stevo nodded. "Yeah, I taught him how to play ball," he said. "He actually made the major leagues. I thought you'd be proud."

Charlie nodded. "I am proud," he whispered. "Proud of both of you."

"He says he is very proud, of both of you."

"Mary, can he hear what I'm saying?" Rosie asked, speaking very loudly.

Charlie shook his head and chuckled. "She hasn't changed a bit."

"Yes, he can hear you, Rosie."

"Coach Thorne, I just wanted to tell you how grateful I am for your example," she said. "I might not have been the best scholar in the group. I

277

certainly wasn't the best chemist. But I learned a lot from you that was more important. I learned about kindness, about integrity and about playing fair. Those lessons have served me well all my life."

"Thank you, Rosie," he said. "You were the ray of sunshine every day I taught you. Thank you for that."

"He said you were his ray of sunshine every day he taught you," Mary said. "And he wanted to thank you for that."

Mary stepped toward the small display. "Your students wanted to show you just how much you meant to them," she said. "When your former students found out what really happened they all wanted to do something to ensure what you did and what you stood for was never forgotten."

"We set up a scholarship with your name on it," Rosie said.

"Actually, Coach, two scholarships," Stevo said, "one for baseball and one for chemistry."

"We want people to know what you did for us for a long, long time," Lo said, wiping away her tears, "because we will never forget."

"Your daughter, Dr. Thorne, is one of the contributors," Mary said. "And when we all gathered this morning to decide on what we were going to do, they all took a moment to share with her how much you touched their lives. Louise told me she realized her father was a hero."

Tears rolled down Charlie's cheeks and he nodded at Mary. "Thank you," he said. "Thank you so much. I can't tell you how much this means to me..."

He turned to the side suddenly and then turned back to Mary. "There's a bright light over there," he said. "I've never seen it before."

Mary wiped the tears from her cheek. "I hate to sound cliché, Charlie, but you need to go to the light."

"Thank you, Mary," he said. "And tell Louise that I always loved her and I'm so proud of her."

"I will," she promised, watching until he faded away.

"He's gone, isn't he?" Rosie asked.

Mary nodded. "Yeah, he's finally gone home."

# Chapter Fifty

Mary came down the stairs slowly, her four-inch heels clicking as she walked. Ian looked up from the cartoon show he and the children were watching. "Good Lord," he gasped. "Quickly tell me the name of my fiancée and why I'm so in love with her."

Mary grinned. "Gillian," she said, "and you love her because she doesn't feel like your sister when you kiss her."

He shook his head. "When you look like that, I'd be fair tempted to try it again."

Mike appeared in the room. "What's all the... Good grief, is it legal for you to go out looking like that?" he bit his knuckle. "If I wasn't already dead, looking at you would have made me die and go to heaven."

"You look like a princess," Maggie said. "But an evil one cause you're wearing black."

"No, you look like an X-Man girl with mutant powers," Andy said. "I bet you could kill people real good."

"You are such flatterers," she said. "And I admit I love every moment of it."

Ian grinned. "Aye, well, you're worthy of each compliment."

"So, when is Bradley supposed to arrive?" Mike asked.

"Any moment now," she said as her phone began to ring.

"Uh, oh, bad sign," Mike said.

"Hello?" Mary said. "A train derailment? Is anyone hurt? Well, that's good. No, no, I can wait. It's not a big deal. Another forty-five minutes, no problem. See you then."

She hung up her phone. "Who derails a train on the Saturday night before Valentine's Day?" she asked.

"Insensitive slob," Mike said. "They should have known you had something planned."

Ian chuckled. "Don't worry, darling, once you see his eyes pop out of his head from just looking at you, it'll be worth the wait."

Mary nodded. "You're right, I mean forty-five minutes, no big deal."

She paced back and forth for a while and finally slipped off her heels.

Forty-five minutes later the phone rang again.

"This can't be good," Mike muttered.

"Hello. No, no, I totally understand. It's your job. People are counting on you. No, really I can wait."

She hung up the phone. "Really? There's no one else in Stephenson County who can help with a train derailment?"

"It's a plot to ruin your date," Ian said. "Do you have an old boyfriend who works for the railroad?"

She snorted. "Be quiet."

Thirty minutes later Mary slipped a big white apron over her dress, took her earrings out of her ears and made her way into the kitchen. "Anyone else want grilled cheese?"

An hour after that, she went upstairs to read the children a bedtime story and got slightly emotional when the clock struck twelve and Cinderella had to leave the ball. "At least she got a chance to go," she muttered.

Once the children had fallen asleep, she left their room. The clock in the hallway displayed 9:15. She went to her bedroom, slipped off her stockings replaced them with thick wool socks.

"Now there's a look I'd thought had gone out of style," Ian said, as she walked down the stairs. "And seeing it in person, I can truly understand why."

She just growled at him.

An hour later, she was dressed in sweats and eating Breyer's Ice Cream from the container. Ian was upstairs working on his computer and Mike was floating somewhere in the house.

"I hate my life," she said sadly, eating another spoonful of Rocky Road.

She shuffled over to the refrigerator and put the ice cream away. Then she climbed back into the recliner, pulled a blanket over herself and turned on "While You Were Sleeping."

# Chapter Fifty-one

A soft buzz woke Mary from a deep sleep. She raised her head and blinked her eyes open, realizing she was asleep in the recliner instead of her own bed. The buzz repeated and she recognized her cell phone was on the vibrate setting. She reached over to the end table, snatched it and answered.

"Hello," she said with a yawn.

"Oh, good, you're awake," Bradley replied from the other end.

Mary shook her head and smiled. "Yes, I'm awake. But just barely."

"What are you wearing?" he asked.

Her eyes widen. "Bradley, this is so not going to be one of those kinds of phone conversations."

His chuckle sent warm feelings through her. "No, nothing like that. But, really, what are you wearing?"

"My CPD sweats," she said with a huff. "My usual nighttime attire."

"Excellent, I was hoping you'd say that," he replied. "I'll be there is ten minutes. Put your running shoes on."

She sat up in the recliner. "Wait. What? It's eleven-thirty at night. I don't understand."

"We have a date."

"But it's eleven-thirty at night," she repeated. "What can we possibly do at eleven-thirty?"

"Mary, trust me," he said simply.

Sighing, she tossed the quilt off and stood up. "Fine, running shoes," she said. "Anything else?"

"A warm coat," he said. "I'll see you soon."

He hung up without giving her another chance to respond. Mary tossed her phone onto the recliner and jogged up the stairs to her room. "Running shoes," she muttered. "Is he nuts?"

"Troubles?" Ian asked, poking his head out of his room.

"No. I'm going out on a date."

He looked her over. She was dressed in baggy sweats, her hair curling around her face in sleepy waves and pink lines across her face from where she laid against the recliner.

"What?" she asked.

"You look lovely," he said. "Lucky's the man who has a chance to date a woman like you."

"That bad, huh?"

Grinning, he started to move back into his room. "Aye, but it's dark outside and the bugger left you waiting for more than four hours."

"Ohhhh," she yelled, darting into her room and rushing for the bathroom.

Glancing into the mirror she saw the marks left by the tufted fabric. "I look like a quilt," she moaned as she splashed warm water on her face and then slathered on moisturizer. "My first official date with Bradley and I look like a waffle."

She patted her face dry, added a little make-up and brushed her hair so it lay in smooth waves over her shoulders. Walking back into her bedroom, she glanced forlornly at the cute little black dress hanging on the outside of the closet. She glanced into the mirror and sighed. "Some girls never get to dress up for the ball."

She pulled some thick white socks out of her dresser drawer, put them on and padded downstairs for her shoes. She was tying her shoes when the front door burst open and Bradley entered.

"Hi," he said, a big smile spreading across his face. "You look wonderful."

"Wonderful?" she asked, looking down at her sweats.

Laughing, he pulled her into his arms and kissed her. "Perfectly wonderful."

She stepped back and stared at him. "You haven't been drinking or exposed to a chemical contaminant have you?"

He shook his head. "No, I'm in control of all of my senses, I promise. Now let's grab your coat and get going. We're running out of time."

"Running out of time?"

"You're spending a lot of time repeating what I'm saying," he pointed out.

"Repeating…"

His raised eyebrow stopped her.

"Fine," she said, grabbing her coat and slipping it on. "Let's go."

The cruiser was at the curb, the engine running. Bradley hurried her into the car, drove down the street to Empire Street and turned left.

"But there aren't any restaurants down this way," Mary said.

Bradley nodded. "We can grab something to eat later," he said. "We have to do this first."

Within minutes they were entering the long drive to Krape Park. "I got special permission to enter the park after hours," he teased. "I know the Chief of Police."

"I hear he's really good looking," Mary said.

"Yeah, I've heard that too," he said, with a grin.

"Too bad his ego is out of control," she replied.

"Well, he hangs around with this gorgeous woman who keeps him in line, so it's really not a problem."

He pulled the car into the parking lot near the band shell. "Okay, ride's over."

He got out of the car and slipped off his overcoat. Mary was surprised to see that he was dressed in sweats and running shoes too.

"What's going on?" she asked.

"I thought we could run a little."

For a moment she couldn't even form words. "You thought that it would be a good idea to go running on a freezing February night at eleven-forty-five p.m.?"

He nodded, clearly unabashed. "You did say I could pick any kind of date I wanted, right?"

She stepped out of the car and took her coat off. "Yes, I did," she said. "So are we racing?"

His mouth spread into a grin. "What else?" he asked, before dashing off toward the path.

"Wait!" she yelled after him, breaking into a run. "I wasn't ready!"

She saw him disappear around the first bend and stopped yelling so she could concentrate on making up for his head start. She scanned the area as she ran, but realized the snow and ice on the ground would hinder any cross-country shortcuts.

Reaching the top of the first hill, she saw his lead wasn't as great as it had been at first. She was catching up with him. She ran down the hill at breakneck speed, hoping she didn't have to stop suddenly. He glanced over his shoulder, saw her coming and increased his speed. However, her downhill momentum was giving her the advantage and she knew she would catch up with him within the next few yards. Suddenly, he veered off the path and headed toward her favorite shortcut, but it required vaulting over two park benches.

"Don't try it, Bradley," she called, her voice lost in the night air. "You'll get hurt."

She ran after him, her shoes slipping on the snow covered field, her breath appearing as puffs of white steam. "Bradley, wait!"

He dashed toward the first bench, grasped the top and vaulted over it without a problem.

*Impressive*, Mary thought, running after him. *But he hasn't won yet.*

Turning to her right, she angled her run downhill, toward the playground. The ground was covered with chunks from recycled tires and would have better traction than the snow. She watched from the corner of her eye as Bradley took the other bench with ease and headed toward the carousel.

She darted through the entrance of the wooden fortress play area. She dashed around the tire run, hopped over the balancing bar and jumped off the edge of the structure, propelling herself toward the carousel from a slightly difference direction.

Her lungs were burning, but she put her all into the last few yards. Glancing over, she could see Bradley was doing the same. Both just feet from their goal, the chain-link fence that surrounded the carousel, she watched in amazement as Bradley threw himself forward and smashed into the fence seconds before she was able to touch it.

"I won," he gasped, as he slid to the frozen ground. "I won."

"You cheated," she panted.

He turned to her and grinned. "Yeah, I know."

Her laugh sounded more like wheezing. "That was a brilliant move."

"I'm sure I learned it from you," he huffed.

"Probably."

"So," he started, turning toward her. "Since I won, I get a prize."

"You admit you cheated and you still want a prize?" she asked, inhaling deeply to catch her breath.

"The prize is why I cheated," he confessed.

"Ah, the ends justify the means?" she asked, raising an eyebrow.

He nodded. "In this case, yes."

"Well, then, I suppose you worked hard enough for it," she said. "What would you like for a prize?"

Snow began to softly fall on them. Big fat flakes that landed on their faces and then melted away. Bradley looked up at the sky and laughed. The full moon appeared from behind a cloud and the snowflakes were suddenly a thousand sparkling points of light. He dug into the pocket of his sweat pants, pulled out a small box and pushed himself up and away from the fence. He knelt on one knee in front of Mary.

"You," he said softly. "You're the prize. Mary O'Reilly, will you marry me?"

He clicked the catch on the lid and held the open box out to her. The diamond ring caught the moonlight and sparkled brilliantly.

Mary shook her head. "But... I don't understand," she stammered.

"I didn't want to ask you on Valentine's Day, everyone does that. I wanted it to be special," he explained, glancing down at his watch. "We made it by three minutes."

"Oh, Bradley," she said, her voice cracking.

"Mary, just say yes," he said, leaning toward her. "That's all you have to do."

She pushed back into the fence. "But there are so many questions we don't have answers to," she said, panic creeping into her voice. "I may never be able to have children. I'm still not over what happened to me. I'm still having flashbacks."

With tears streaming down her face, she jumped to her feet and slowly stepped backwards. "I'm sorry, Bradley. I just can't."

She turned and ran away from him, knowing the path before her was mirroring her future; dark, cold and alone.

# Chapter Fifty-two

Mary had taken about five steps when a hand clapped down on her shoulder, stopping her midstride.

"No," was all Bradley said.

She took a deep shaky breath and swallowed back her tears. "Bradley, I really can't…"

"I won the race, I get the prize," he said simply. "No."

She twirled around, anger and hurt replacing sadness. "This isn't a game," she hissed.

Then she saw his face; calm, serious and determined.

"No, you're damn right, this isn't a game," he said softly. "This is our lives."

"But I told you why…" she began.

"But you didn't give me a chance to respond. You gave me your reasons, fair enough, but now you have to listen to me."

She wiped her arm across her face, brushing away her tears, and nodded.

"You're right, I want children," he said. "But the only children I dream of are the ones we have together. The only child I want is one who is nurtured and loved by both of us. If we can't have children of our own, then we can adopt. I don't want a child if you're not the mother."

He pulled her gently into his arms. "I need you in my life, Mary. You hold my heart in your hand. If you walk away, you walk away with my heart. I'll never be whole again."

Crying softly, she laid her head against his shoulder and placed her hands on his chest. *This was not fair*, she thought. *I'm trying to do the right thing for both of us. I'm trying to protect him. Why can't he see that?*

He lightly rubbed her back and laid his head on hers. "Mary," he whispered. "What are you worrying about now?"

"But what if…if I can't…?" she began.

"I told you that I was not going to ever let fear and doubt stand in the way of our love," he interrupted. "I'm more afraid of facing life without you than I am of helping you work through the flashbacks."

He placed his hands on her shoulders and leaned back, meeting her eyes. "Our love has been strong enough to overcome obstacles much bigger than this. You have to have a little more faith in both of us."

She thought about what he'd said and realized that he was right. She had let fear rule her life lately, instead of faith. She'd nearly let Gary win again. When in the hell had she turned into such a wimp? An O'Reilly never runs from a good fight!

Taking a deep breath, she met his eyes. "You cheated," she said.

Relief spread over his face and he grinned down at her. "Darn right and I'd do it again."

"I have to admit, it was a pretty impressive run," she said.

"It was the most important race of my life," he replied seriously. "And I won."

She shook her head and watched the happiness leave his eyes for a moment. "No, I won," she said softly, as she reached up and kissed him softly on the lips.

He wrapped his arms tightly around her and lifted her off the ground, spinning in a circle as the snow flew around them. Then he kissed her until she was breathless. "Say it," he insisted, lowering her feet to the ground, but keeping his arms firmly around her. "Please say it."

"I love you, Bradley Alden," she said, her eyes glowing with love. "And, yes, I will marry you."

# Chapter Fifty-three

The sun was barely up when Ian came down the stairs to the kitchen. Mary was already busy in the kitchen. He stopped at the bottom of the stairs and sniffed the air. "What is it that we'd be having for breakfast this morning?" he asked.

"Waffles," Mary said, with a quick smile.

"Waffles?" he repeated. "That's a fine way to greet the day. Are we celebrating?"

Mary tried to hide her smile, but the joy she was feeling was too great to hold in.

"Yes," she said with a wide grin. "Yes, we certainly are celebrating."

"Ach, do you think you'll be hurting the wee bairns' feelings acting this way?" he asked.

"What? What do you mean?"

"Oh, that's right, I dinna tell you," he said. "While you were getting ready for your fancy date last night, Katie called. They were getting in late last night and would be coming over this morning to pick up Andy and Maggie."

"Oh," she said, her light mood slightly diminished. "Oh, well, I'm going to miss them."

"Aye, like a splinter," Ian teased.

"Come on," she said. "Admit it; you loved every moment of it."

He nodded, straddling the kitchen chair, and looking longingly up stairs. "Andy's full of wit and Maggie, well she's wrapped my heart around her wee finger."

"Do we really have to give them back?" she asked.

He chuckled. "Aye, I'm sure Katie's just as fond of them," he said. "So, if we aren't celebrating being free and single once again, what are we celebrating?"

She held her left hand out, displaying her new engagement ring. "Not being single," she said.

Ian got up, walked over and took her hand in his. "Well, look at this shiny rock," he said. "But it's no competition to the sparkle in your eyes. I ken you're happy."

"So happy," she admitted.

"Aye," he said. "And it's about time."

She laughed. "Yes it is."

The sound of small footsteps on the stairs was almost bittersweet.

"Guess what, Mary?" Maggie said. "My mom is coming home today."

"That is so wonderful," Mary said. "I'm sure she missed you."

Maggie nodded. "Yes, I'm sure she missed me too."

Ian laughed and ruffled her hair. "What do you think about waffles?"

Her eyes widened. "Really? Waffles? I love waffles."

Ian pulled some plates from the cabinet and set them on the counter. "Well, we're celebrating this morning," he said. "So we're all having waffles."

"Do you want butter and syrup or strawberries and whipped cream?" Mary asked her.

"How about..." she said, lengthening the word as she made up her mind. "Both."

Ian laughed out loud. "Aye, darling, you can have both."

Andy hurried down the stairs carrying his suitcase and his backpack. "My mom is coming to get us today," he announced. "I told her we could stay longer, but she said she missed us too much."

"Well, I can understand that," Mary said. "I'm going to miss you when you're gone."

Andy slipped onto a chair at the table. "I could come over every day and eat breakfast with you," he offered. "So you wouldn't miss me so much."

Mary grinned. "Well, we need to work something out with your mother, so we get to see you more often," she agreed.

"I like your ring," Maggie said, as she stuffed her mouth with waffle.

"Thank you," Mary replied. "Bradley gave it to me."

Andy stopped buttering his waffle for a moment and looked up at her. "Are you guys getting married?" he asked, delighted.

Mary nodded. "Yes we are."

"That is so cool," Andy said.

"Why, thank you, Andy," Mary said, a little surprised at his reaction.

"So, he's going to move here, right?" he asked. "Chief Alden is going to be my neighbor?"

Ian laughed. "Now I see why he's so excited."

"Well, it's okay," Mary said. "I can totally understand his infatuation."

A little while later, both of the children were washed up and ready to go.

"Your mom will be here in a moment," Mary said, blinking back tears. "Thank you for staying with me."

Maggie came over and gave her a big hug. "You are my favoritist place to stay," she said. "I love you."

"I love you too, Maggie," she said, returning the hug.

Ian squatted down and Maggie hugged him too. "Remember now," Ian said, his voice cracking slightly. "You promised you're going to marry me when you're older."

"Will you get me a pretty ring, like Mary's?"

Laughing, he gave her a quick squeeze, "Aye, just like Mary's."

Andy walked over to Mary. "I guess I'm too old for a hug, right?"

Mary shook her head. "Well, you might be too old," she said. "But I'm not."

She gave him a hug.

"I'm glad the Chief is marrying you," he whispered to her. "He's like a hero."

Nodding, she wiped away a few stray tears. "Yeah, he is."

When she heard the knock on the door, she gave Andy another quick hug and stood up. "I think that might be for you," she said.

She opened the door and Katie came inside. The children threw themselves against her. "Mom, you're home!"

Katie hugged them and held them for a few moments. "I missed both of you so much," she said. "Did you behave yourselves?"

Maggie nodded. "I was so good. And guess what? Mary got a ring from Bradley. She's getting married."

Katie looked up at Mary. "Really?" she asked. "That's wonderful."

"Yeah, Chief Alden is going to be living here," Andy said. "That's so cool."

Katie laughed. "Yes, that is cool," she agreed.

"Can I go tell Dad?" Andy asked.

"Yes, you may," Katie said.

"Me too?" Maggie asked.

"Yes, but be sure to say thank you and goodbye to Mary and Ian."

"Thank you. Goodbye," both children repeated obediently as they rushed out the door.

"Well, I love emotional goodbyes," Ian laughed. "Katie they were a delight. Sometime we'll have to tell you about Maggie's guardian angel."

"I'd love to hear more about him," she said.

"Aye, I'm sure you will," he said. "Now, I'll go and clean up the waffles. Welcome home, Katie."

"Waffles?" she said to Mary. "You really did spoil them."

"It was my pleasure. Really."

Katie took Mary's hand and looked at the ring. "Oh, well, that's just beautiful," she said. "And was it romantic?"

Mary grinned. "It was perfect," she said.

"Daddy!" They both heard Maggie's cry of delight and peeked out the door to see Maggie throw herself into her father's arms.

A shadow of sadness passed over Mary's face.

"What's wrong?" Katie asked.

Mary shrugged. "Nothing really."

Katie laughed. "You're not a very good liar, Mary. Now tell me."

"I don't know if Bradley and I will be able to have children," she said. "I don't know if I'll ever be able to be a mother."

Katie hugged Mary. "My mother always told me never to borrow troubles," she said. "Just wait and see what happens, you might be just fine and you've worried for nothing."

"Mom, come on," Andy yelled.

Mary smiled. "You're right, and you'd better get going."

She squeezed Mary's hand. "Things will turn out the way they are supposed to," she said, moving to the door. "Besides, there's always adoption."

Mary walked with Katie out to the porch. She nodded. "I know," she said. "But I've always wondered about that."

Katie hugged her again. "It's a wonderful experience," she said softly. "I know because our sweet Maggie is adopted."

## About the author:

Terri Reid lives near Freeport, the home of the Mary O'Reilly Mystery Series, and loves a good ghost story. She lives in a hundred-year-old farmhouse complete with its own ghost. She loves hearing from her readers at author@terrireid.com.

## Books by Terri Reid:

Loose Ends – A Mary O'Reilly Paranormal Mystery (Book One)

Good Tidings – A Mary O'Reilly Paranormal Mystery (Book Two)

Never Forgotten – A Mary O'Reilly Paranormal Mystery (Book Three)

Final Call – A Mary O'Reilly Paranormal Mystery (Book Four)

Darkness Exposed – A Mary O'Reilly Paranormal Mystery (Book Five)

Natural Reaction – A Mary O'Reilly Paranormal Mystery (Book Six)

Secret Hollows – A Mary O'Reilly Paranormal Mystery (Book Seven)

Broken Promises – A Mary O'Reilly Paranormal Mystery (Book Eight)

Twisted Paths – A Mary O'Reilly Paranormal Mystery (Book Nine)

Veiled Passages – A Mary O'Reilly Paranormal Mystery (Book Ten)

Bumpy Roads – A Mary O'Reilly Paranormal Mystery (Book Eleven)

The Ghosts Of New Orleans – A Paranormal
Research and Containment Division (PRCD) Case
File

Made in the USA
Lexington, KY
12 April 2014